Praise for the
Wren's Song Series

"This book is unapologetically raw. Stripping passion down to its most primal, snarling, clawing best. Do not miss this delectable morsel from one of the most deviously talented authors I know" ~ Zoe Blake, USA Today bestselling author

"Electrifying, dark and delicious--I devoured every tantalizing word of this devious tale." ~ Renee Rose, USA Today bestselling author

"Cain's storytelling is hypnotic and fascinating. Such an imaginative story that had me engrossed from beginning to end." ~ Alta Hensley, USA Today bestselling author

BRANDED

WREN'S SONG, BOOK ONE

ADDISON CAIN

1

———

"Accept my seed, Omega."

The breath wafting over her cheek was rancid, but it was the last thing Wren might take stock of when that *thing* was cracking her pelvis in half. She had done as she'd been instructed. Remained docile when the man had yanked her legs embarrassingly wide over his thighs. She had even ignored the thick thatch of coarse salt and pepper hair on his chest scratching her back when he hoisted her up.

He'd growled as her mother told her he

would, and torn through her barrier with one impatient yank of her hips. Unable to scream, Wren had only arched her spine, head thrown back on his shoulder. The Alpha, either oblivious or uncaring for her comfort, grasped her hips, bobbing her up and down his veined cock three times. With the fourth rude shunt, he'd clawed at her softer places and driven her down until her cheeks slapped against his lap. Immediately something ballooned inside aching guts. It pressed her bladder to the point Wren was certain she'd dribbled more than a little piss on her new mate, continuing to expand until squished bowels, organs, and jangled nerves all screamed for relief.

"Damn you, Omega. Take my seed!"

Take what where? She didn't understand what she was supposed to do now.

At her back, the stranger panted, shifting beneath her as if he too were extremely uncomfortable. When she failed to perform, his irritation quickly translated into anger. The stink invaded Wren's nostrils, it made her skin buzz.

Angry Alphas killed.

Angry Alphas must always be appeased.

Staring forward across the dimly lit, yet finely appointed space, Wren inhaled and exhaled on a count of three. There was nothing to be done about the stinging stretch where her legs were hooked over the man's spread thighs. He had not offered to take her to a bed or even asked to see her build a nest. No, the couch in his fine house's receiving room had suited his purpose well enough.

Examine and test the stock.

Fuck the virgin with her father on the other side of the cracked door.

The man who'd brought his Omega daughter to sell listening to this. To the Alpha's strained breaths, to his grunts and wheezing.

Her father was listening to her failure.

Wren forced herself to look down. She had not seen the Alpha's cock before he'd shunted it unexpectedly into her, or even had a good look at the male. Her eyes had been downcast when they arrived, lest her father strike her for insolence. She had disrobed for inspection. She had moved as commanded and not resisted when the Alpha yanked her to the nearest seat.

And her father had exited the room to listen so he might claim full payment for what transpired.

Payment for... *this*. Wren stared where only the root of an Alpha cock was visible stretching her labia beyond imagining. There was a little blood, far less than she'd anticipated considering the burn. The red spread with their fluids, matting the hair that peppered his swollen ball sack.

The knot in her belly gave an angry pulse, expanding again in a bid to ruin her completely. Gnashing his teeth, the Alpha almost whined against her neck, his balls thundering in twitching pulses. They too expanded, the skin under all that coarse hair growing shiny and white from the stretch.

"Fucking Omega…" A meaty hand left her hip, landing on her belly as if that might force her even further down his meat. But there was nowhere else to go. She was tied to him by that pulsating knot spreading agony in her guts. From the way he fought to speak, how his breath hitched in a whine with each breath, the Alpha was in as much pain as she. "You have one purpose. Milk my fucking cock!"

If that knot kept banging against her pubic bone, she was going to be sick all over his rug. Stalled, unsure what it was he wanted from her, Wren thought the wisest course was to remain still and wait.

It was the wrong choice.

"Your freak daughter is failing to comply!" The snarled shout was directed to the cracked door.

The meek response was never the tone

Wren's father took with her. "Have you… umm… stimulated her, sir?"

Wren's new owner turned his head, yelling so sharply the girl flinched. "Of course I have! She belligerently refuses to bring me to orgasm. My fucking knot is full. Gah—" Slick with sweat, the Alpha squeezed her tighter, caught in a waving cramp of his own. "I'll have your goddamn head for this, Carson!"

"Wren, honey." Through the cracked door, her father sing-songed, "Relax and take his seed. Show this illustrious Alpha you wish to serve as his mate."

She wanted to sign that I didn't understand, to reach out for the man who'd brought her there to sell her. But he could not see.

Her potential mate roared, "SEND IN HELENA!"

Another door in the chilly room opened, a woman in a vivid robe rushing forward. "How can I serve you, my Alpha?"

"Bend over the desk and wait for me!"

Wren watched the woman quickly strip, viewing another naked female body for the first time in her life. With no preamble, the pretty brunette bent at the waist, the globes of her ass presented, her cheek to the wood.

Beta female parts were on display.

Cruel fingers reached for Wren's stretched labia, the Alpha yanking at the sensitive flesh as he grunted and threw her forward with his weight. His ballooning testicles doubled in size, the man groaning with the worst sort of agony.

His pain was nothing to hers. The knot that was meant to tie them together in life was deformed by his tricks until it could be pulled free of her body. Wren was dumped on the floor, hand pressed between her trembling legs as she wailed.

From the corner of her eye, she watched the Alpha scythe his cock into the waiting female, wrecking her with the madness of his need to release. Unlike Wren, the Beta gave him immediate relief, the Alpha's cry ear-splitting.

Bowed over, curled in on herself, Wren shut her eyes to it all.

When her father was called forward, even then she refused to rise to meet his gaze. Naked and shamed on the floor of a stranger's house, she sniffed, wishing she couldn't hear the terrible things that were said about her.

"Was she not trained?"

"My wife took great pains to explain what would be expected, sir. You have my humblest apologies that she failed, but if you are not going to take her as your new mate, you still owe for the tearing of her hymen. She will be harder to sell unintact."

Of course her father would try to weasel credits from this man…

The Alpha gave an incredulous laugh. "Your mute albino freak might be pretty to look at, but she is the worst fuck imaginable. If you think I'd expose that cunt to another Alpha in this city, you're wrong."

"You owe me one-thousand credits for her virginity!" Her father never once came to her defense, never offered her comfort, he only tried to squeeze what he could from a far richer man. "The contract was clear. No matter the outcome of the first mating, a fee will be paid!"

The sound of ice hitting the side of crystal, the pour of liquor. Far calmer, the Alpha took a long sip. "The contract," a smile in his voice, the Alpha purred, "is null and void if the merchandise is defective. You get nothing, Carson. She will be tagged and dumped in the Warrens and you will leave here grateful to be breathing."

No! Ignoring sore muscles and the screaming pain between her legs, Wren scampered to her father and wrapped her arm around his leg. Signing frantically, she begged him for mercy.

He looked down at his pale, violet-eyed child, deadpan as he said, "I should have had you euthanized at birth."

2

―――――

The bones in her back cracked splendidly when Wren straightened from a low crouch. The city might be enjoying the heat of summer, but the Warrens were always ice-cold—the kind of chill that locked up muscle and joints. And with that chill came disease-riddled damp.

Medicine was damn expensive.

Even now there was a rattle in her lungs. But it wasn't the killing kind. A good day or two in a dry room and she'd cough up the phlegm and be right as rain.

Would it be nice to peel out of mud soaked boots and let her toes de-prune? Yes, but that would have to wait. She had sloshed down to the pump-yard for a reason more important than clean air and dry socks.

Coughing into her fist, she worked out as much of the lung rot as she could. Once she dropped down into the pipes, she couldn't risk so much as a wheeze. Not until she found the one called Caspian.

It was a hard enough life in the Warrens without men like Caspian intruding to make it all the worse. His syndicate offered *honest* work. His lackeys tempted those new to this hellhole, those who had yet to learn better, with food and a dry bed, roping them into slavery.

Wren spit on the name.

She'd spit on the man if it wouldn't mean her neck. And where would that leave her boys?

Dead.

Villains, powermongers, and innocent

fools were cast into the muck every day. To people like Wren, it was nothing… changed nothing. Honestly, at this point, it was hard enough keeping little bellies full without having to give a damn about the men who came and went.

City scourges and cracking walls. Sinking buildings and floating bodies.

Nothing and no one was going to change the Warrens.

But that was beside the point.

The land sunk deeper every day; staying ahead of the bog was all that mattered.

And love.

Family.

Family mattered most.

Wren would drag hers away from Caspian's Syndicate kicking and screaming if she had to. She knew the scoundrels well enough. Alec and Mikael had simply gone down the pipes for the laughs…

Gone down and never came back.

Both were crafty little monkeys, capable

and knowledgeable of the channels. Both had the skill to slip away unseen if they'd been spying or dumb enough to steal from Alphas. *But they had not returned.*

Street kids knew better than to fall for the rumors of Caspian's power. The boys had lived their whole lives in a constant state of circumspection, and did not need food or shelter beyond what their family, what Wren, might provide. Unless one of *the shifts* had sunk the city's monumental skyscrapers deeper into the Warrens' muck and drowned them while they played.

To even think it…

No. They would be here with Caspian.

They had to be.

And Wren needed to know if they were prisoners, or simply wanted to play with the big boys for kicks.

And so she waded through the mud, aware that a single tremor might change the drift of rotting refuse and suck her down like it did so many every day. She went into the dark, flipping up her goggles once the sun was doused by metal tubes.

The sun had never been her friend.

Perhaps that's why she had thrived in the Warrens since her father had dropped her here years ago. All the way down here, the buildings were too tall to offer more than the hazy afterthought of light.

Every day the city sunk a little deeper. And every day up top, they built higher and higher to escape the inevitable mud.

The very mud that was fighting to suck her boot from her foot.

In the distance, Wren could hear the sound of rushing water, a sign she was closer to the pipeworks than she'd thought.

She wanted to pretend it was nothing, that she wasn't afraid. But she was. Alphas put things inside a body and tore them out. Alphas were the reason her right cheek had been tattooed with the symbol for defective merchandise.

Wren had never met a single one without

a black heart. And those condemned to the Warrens were the worst of the worst.

A pinpoint of light showed the outlet of her stagnant pipe, the roar of rushing water warning her that trouble lay ahead. Creeping, mud up to her chin, Wren counted to three, over and over, and refused to think of anything beyond the fact her boys needed her.

A room so bright with electric light that she had to lower her goggles to see anything at all. Astounded, she took it all in, failing completely to accept what she saw. *Hundreds* of men moved through ancient drainage systems. A rough looking bunch; men she would not like to see following her down a dark alley.

Men marked with the dark print of a hand over their mouths—Caspian's mark—held forbidden tech. Weapons. Circling the workers, less guard and more taskmaster.

What the hell had her boys gotten themselves into?

And yes, they were here. As were many

other children Wren had somehow never seen before.

Frowning, she leaned back on her heels, mud squishing in sodden socks. Many of the little ones looked scared. Alec and Mikael were among them, dirty… well, they were *always* dirty… but drenched through. Mikael was clearly sick… hacking where he lay sweating despite the cold.

But what left her jaw gaping was why they were wet.

Fresh water poured from the walls, raining down upon the workers as if it were cheap and easy to find.

Clean, clear water.

She was so screwed.

Sucking in a deep, mist-drenched breath, Wren scanned the aqueducts and saw the kingpin himself. Like all Alphas, his size was intimidating. Caspian: ugly, brawny, vicious…

She'd once heard a rumor that he wore a coat made from the skins of his enemies. At the time, Wren had laughed. Seeing the beast now, she wasn't so much as cracking a smirk.

It was flesh colored, if flesh had been tanned and stretched. A patchwork of various shades sewn with skill and absolutely disgusting.

3

"We have an intruder wading through Pitchfork Canal 7, sir."

Caspian refused to look away from his data relay. There were more important items on the agenda than another starving asshole stumbling down to see things not meant for their eyes. "Kill them."

Kieran radioed the order. "That is an affirmative. Shoot the—" The relay cut him off. "What?"

Lowering his arm, Caspian looked to his

subordinate, annoyed with the interruption, and cocked a brow.

"It seems, sir, it's a child." More radio babble chimed at Kieran's ear. "He's approaching the boys on the third floor now."

They turned in unison to look over the rim of the pipeworks, and found the intruder marching boldly toward the child laborers. A rather exuberant gutter rat jumped up upon seeing him, waving both thin arms in the air. More boys took notice, many leaving their posts to rush over and see who'd come to play.

Their enthusiasm was short-lived, the mud soaked stranger wrenching one of the children by the ear until most of them scattered. It would have been funny had that same man not reached down for another boy, hoisting him over his shoulder like a sack of flour.

This one who thought to steal his workers, was blatantly shuffling off with two.

"Have him brought here." Caspian leveled

the command at Kieran just in time to witness the figure approaching of his own accord.

Under the shadow of a hood, the shine of wide eyes betrayed the stranger's anxiety. The interloper shifted the weight of the coughing child on his shoulder, the drape of his clothing catching on… well, well, *breasts*.

It was *a woman* covered in all that mud, not a young boy at all.

And she, in all her infinite stupidity, was looking him right in the eye.

Caspian smirked, noting he was not the only male to take notice of what had crept into their midst. There were shifts in posture in the men around him, murmurs…

Raw meat. A mud-caked Warrens rat who probably smelled of rotting towels and tasted of sewage. Not worth throwing to his men.

This weakling she-rat was struggling up the stairs, trying to manage the weight of the limp child—dragging along a second, less obedient boy in her wake.

And what did she see when she looked at

him? Caspian's smirk grew meaner. She saw the male who was going to end her for daring to touch *his* property.

And still she marched, huffing for air by the time she reached his platform.

Just as he thought. A Warrens rat dressed in her finest rags, dripping with refuse and stinking of the shit she'd waded through. A hood covered whatever tangled—likely lice infested—mop she might have, but it didn't cover the mark on her cheek. *Defective.*

Stark black ink on snowy white skin. Just as her lashes and eyebrows were snowy white.

They looked clean against all the filth, framing eyes an impossible shade of lavender.

So that's why she'd been cast into the mud…

A hacking cough unsettled the boy on her shoulder. Easing him down, she held his head to her breast and gave three hard raps to his back. Her second companion didn't seem to notice, the kid staring up at Caspian with awe.

The woman let out a sigh, giving the Alpha her full attention.

And said nothing.

She was waiting for him to speak, completely candid in expression as if it was he who intruded on her. Yet those eyes said that she knew fucking well that she should not have been there.

She was frightened, the scent of fear seeping just enough through the muck drenching her to mark the air.

As well she fucking should be! Rolling his neck in a quick snap of motion, bones popped, Caspian releasing a growl. "And you would be?"

Breaking their gaze, she turned to the gaping boy. When he failed to pay attention, she grabbed him by the scruff of the neck and gave him a good, hard shake.

Brushing off her grip, his face went red as he grumbled, "She's Jax, I'm Alec and that's Mikael."

Expressive, earnest eyes went back to Caspian. She nodded.

Arms crossing the span of Caspian's chest, he sneered. "I didn't ask the boy, I asked you."

"Her brain can't make words, sir. Only sounds," Alec piped up, throwing his shoulders back in a mirror image of the man before him.

She stroked her hand down Alec's tangled hair before pointing at the coughing boy clutched to her breast. Then she thumbed at her own chest before moving her hand in a circle as if to signify they were together.

"You wish to take these boys with you?"

A quick nod was offered.

"No."

His growled reply did not discourage her as it should have.

The female silently assessed, breathed, blinked, and waited.

"I said no," Caspian repeated himself, a

thing he never did and would make her pay for.

Jax smirked, a stifled breath coming forth.

Had she just laughed at him?

Yes. The slow curl of her lips hinted at the beginnings of a smile. Not quite as collected as she wished to appear, a drop of sweat dripped down her temple, running through the grime on her cheek as she began to sign with one hand.

"She wants to trade," Alec interpreted, clearly dejected at the idea. "But I don't think you should let us go. I like it here."

She smacked the kid upside the back of the head hard enough to rattle him a step forward.

"I do, Jax! I like it here!" Pride wounded, the kid threw a glare at his would-be savior. "Look at all the water! We're allowed to drink as much as we want."

Fingers flying, she spelled out words Caspian couldn't begin to grasp. An argument commenced between woman and child, halting abruptly when the fevered boy at her breast drew a rattled breath and said, "I want to go home."

The female purred an instant offer of comfort, turning her full attention on the ill child. Smoothing back the sweat soaked spikes of his hair, she cooed, even pressed her lips to his brow.

And there it was. A declaration of her intention.

A fucking Omega. *Here.*

Purring like a kitten over a raggedy boy in a room full of Alpha killers. Was she fucking mental? "Do you have a death wish, woman?"

In her arms, the boy coughed all the harder until wheezes turned into pathetic sobs.

Violet eyes darted in their sockets, landing on Caspian as if it were his fault the child cried and clung.

She was hardly more than child herself, but… "Is that your offspring, Omega?"

The other boy lost the awe in his eyes, glaring at the Alpha who'd threatened his companion. "She's Jax! Don't call her Omega!"

Caspian rounded on Alec, terrible and deadly. "Another word from you, *boy*, and I'll toss you over the railing. You can drink all the water you like as you drown in it."

The woman hooked an arm around the loud-mouthed child, her palm fast against his mouth. With her interpreter silenced, she was left with nothing but those accusing eyes and the ability to nod.

She shook her head no.

"No, he is not your offspring?"

Arms full, she turned her face to display the mark again.

"An orphan dumped here like you were?"

An emphatic nod. There was a magic to the movement of her expression. With a lingering look and a few moments of emotion, she wordlessly said that to give her this child would be in his favor… the little one was sick. Sickness would spread in the damp and weaken his workers.

One quick solution solved this problem. Caspian grinned. "We could just kill him."

Jax gave a small agreeable shrug, but followed it with a hard look. *"But we both know that would be more trouble than letting me take them home."*

"I've never seen an Omega rampage. It might be great entertainment..." But not worth the cleanup. Set one into a protective bloodlust and Omegas lost the ability to feel pain, to register fear... to do anything but mindlessly protect their young. She'd die, of course. But so might some of his men.

Dead Omegas, *even defective ones*, were not good for morale. At least one of the men standing at his back would have a soft spot for a ballsy woman who wanted to keep a couple of kids away from people like him.

She mouthed the word, *trade*.

Caspian spread his arms, entertained. "And what could you possibly trade to me for the lives of two vagrant children? Water? Credits? Power?"

Tech.

"Salvage?" Caspian was almost impressed with how *unimpressive* her offer was.

A hint of a smile creased the skin beside the woman's eyes. Nodding enthusiastically, she hugged her boys tighter.

This Jax was going to be sorely disappointed. Omegas only had one commodity to trade in. Cunt. "Lead the way."

4
———————

Not once had the ponderous Alpha rocking the sinking planks with his heft offered to help manage Mikael's weight. Wren hadn't expected him too, but she had struggled keeping her temper every time he barked at her to walk faster. It was difficult enough to keep one's footing when every walkway was half-sunken in mud. Harder still to walk those unstable paths carrying a ten-year-old.

He wasn't supposed to have come with her. Shit. Caspian was *the* Big Bad with better things to do. But Alec had opened his mouth, like the smartass adolescent he was, and made her truly mute. How could she describe her wares?

The brute didn't understand signs. She didn't have pen or paper.

Those rare and valuable things were back in her den where the rot couldn't get them.

As was everything she owned. Should the Alpha choose to take it all… all of them would starve.

She didn't even want to think of burying more little bodies in the muck.

Continuing to grip Alec by the scruff of his neck, her fingers tangled in his uncut hair —a leash to keep him from wandering back off to the pipeyard and an early death.

He was going to be the death of her first.

And boy was Alec angry with her for ruining his fun. His anger she could handle. What was really worrying was his embarrassment. Embarrassed teenage boys did stupid things to prove they were men.

The cute, stupid little idiot would get himself killed if she couldn't secure Caspian's word that she owned both children now.

Owned, because that is how he most certainly viewed them.

His syndicate, *The* syndicate in the Warrens was the one thing you always, *always*, avoided. Once in, there was no out. They fed off the wretches, kept them poor, kept them addicted, and kept them *employed*. Enslaved.

Caspian was going to bleed her dry.

He was going to know where she nested.

A man like him had not come all this way for a few dehumidifiers and rebuilt water filtration.

Gut gnawing anxiety left her sweating. Exactly what she needed when she was already soaked through and disgusting.

The male's callously rattled growl warned, "I don't have all day."

Before she could stop herself, she threw him a glare saying, *"Then why the fuck didn't you send someone else to barter on your behalf?"*

"I've killed men with my bare hands for daring to look at me that way."

The beast thought this was funny? Of course he did. Sadist.

Picking up the pace, the stitch in her side warped from a minor annoyance to tried and true pain. Mikael squirmed as he coughed, and she felt his weight slip off her shoulder. Head first he went, right down to the planks.

And then the body stopped, forehead inches away from impact.

Wren's ass met splintered wood when her balance failed. Biting back a groan, she gulped down stink-riddled atmosphere and saw just why Mikael seemed to float in midair. The Alpha had him by the ankle, and the brute looked disturbed by the fact.

Clambering to her aching feet, Wren reached out, signaling she was ready for Caspian to pass the boy forward.

The Alpha curled a lip, openly hostile as

he snarled, "Your attempt to impress me with your stubbornness has been noted. Move!"

Sorely tempted to make a grab for her boy, Wren fisted her hands. Fear infected her expression, she was even foolish enough to feel her eyes well.

"It's the cough that will kill him. Not me." The Alpha turned the child right side up, flinging him over his shoulder carelessly. "March."

Fast as she could manage in squashing shoes and with a petulant teen at her side, Wren hobbled over the planks, bringing the wolf right to her door.

A hand-hewn sign above read: *Goods For Sale*. It creaked in the drafts, reminding her to hurry with the locks before even more Warrens dwellers saw just who'd followed her home.

No one would frequent her shop if the head of The Syndicate was seen here.

One lock, two. Five. Seven, and the door gave, Wren falling inward after it in her haste to get inside. Alec rushed past her, Caspian ducking his head to fit past her door.

Like clockwork she slammed the door shut and locked it tight, letting out a breath when the last tumbler clicked. Flipping the switch on the nearest dehumidifier, Wren hastily stole Mikael away from a man she was certain would drop him out of spite.

Zippers were yanked, buttons popped, sodden clothes pulled from a rail-thin body. All done on the entry floor until a naked boy curled in on himself, shivering.

And he wasn't the only naked child. Alec had stripped to his skivvies, arms out to help his friend to the bathing room. But as he helped his brother, he shot Wren an angry glare.

She was not forgiven.

Wren had much to say on the subject, but kept her lips sealed, so to speak, so she might deal with her *guest*.

"Your home is"—making no attempt to

hide his disgust, the Alpha surveyed what her hard work had achieved—"very clean."

Well, it had been before the four of them had dragged in an ocean of mud. Considering it was full of dry air and that there was even some decent salvaged furniture, Wren wasn't sure what he had to complain about. Lost wonders she'd personally fished out of the muck were everywhere. Working view monitors, music receptacles, she even had a rickety cleaning bot.

Of course, the boys all had their favorite device, a working game console that might fetch her a pretty penny if she found the right buyer. Unfortunately, kids' entertainment devices didn't sell much in the Warrens.

Kids rarely survived here. Not on their own… and that's how they arrived.

Rubbing heat into her hands, Wren breathed into cupped palms and eyeballed the man who seemed to be stealing the little ones before she could get to them.

Bastard.

"What did I tell you about looking at me that way?"

Throwing back her hood, she signed, aware he would have no clue as to her meaning. *"That you'd kill me you vile, disgusting, piece of half-rotted dog."*

The man instead narrowed his eyes. His attention went to the knot of white hair pinned atop her head, his massive hand taking a grip of her shoulder. "I have a feeling you deserve punishment for whatever it was you just said."

Wren smiled, all warmth and hospitality for the brute as she signed, *"Let's get this over with."*

"Take off your coat." Meaty fingers started yanking at her zipper, careless for tearing the only slicker she had. "What else are you hiding under the world's ugliest garments?"

Just because the boys knew to strip and wash as soon as they entered, didn't mean Wren was going to do the same. But the beast had her out of her covering, spinning and twisting her about until she slipped on the busted tile floor and fell.

Gaping, she cradled a tweaked wrist, left with a wet flannel shirt that clung to her breasts.

"Up with you." Caspian caught her as she tried to scramble back, setting the frazzled thing to her feet. With a grip of iron around her arm, his eyes raked over what little he'd uncovered. Then he drew her flailing body flush to run his nose up her neck. "You think I would have heard of a pretty, albino whore working the Warrens. How much do you sell for?"

Slapping at him, she pressed back with what little strength her arms had left.

"Too proud for me?" The man chuckled; it was not a noise of mirth. It was one of vile thoughts and vicious anger. "My face might be a bit banged up, but you'll scream for my knot like a good little Omega slut. Play nice, and I might let you keep your boys."

Wren squealed when he licked his lips, poking the tattooed flesh of her cheek. *Defective*.

Caspian's brow dipped dangerously low. "Diseases?"

Head shaking, Wren patted his chest in a bid to be set free.

"What're you doing to her?" Alec—wiped clean, and dressed fresh—with Mikael leaning on him for support, shouted, "She ain't no whore!"

He eyeballed the boys but made no move to put Wren down. "She got a mate?"

Looking skyward as if it was a stupid question, Alec said, "Who do you think dumped her here?"

"Roll your eyes again at me, boy, and I'll pop them right out of their sockets." When the teen showed the wisdom of fear, Caspian demanded more, "Explain."

"The Alpha gave her a poke and didn't like her. He had her marked so she couldn't be sold to anyone else."

Red up to her roots, Wren looked away, thoroughly humiliated that Alec knew such things.

The bulging arms at her back softened, Wren sliding down a stone-hard chest until her feet hit the puddle of mud on the floor.

The interrogation wasn't done. Pinching her chin, Caspian watched her eyes very closely. "You're raw?"

She didn't understand and it was clear in her expression.

"A virgin?"

Lavender eyes darted to where Alec stood, Wren wishing with all her heart the boys were not in the room.

"He stays until I say so." The pressure on her chin increased. "Answer me."

She shook her head no. She was not a virgin.

"Just the one time?"

An embarrassed nod.

"Then you're raw." A mean grin broke across Caspian's face. "And you might actually have something worth bartering for here if what's hiding under these clothes is as pretty as that hair."

Wren drew in a deep, shaky breath, blowing it out slowly in a bid to compose herself. All of this had gone so far out of hand, she didn't have a clue how to unravel it.

"I like pretty things that like me. I like pretty things that obey." He ran a finger over her jaw, her pink lips, inspecting the merchandise as he enticed with an Alpha growl. "Be a good girl, now, and parlay. Do you want those boys or not?"

Signing carefully so Alec might answer, Wren shared her greatest shame. "The Alpha... I..." How the fuck does one describe what happened that night? "I didn't know how to take his seed. It hurt him. He hurt me. I'm defective..."

Hearing Alec repeat what she'd shared, Wren began to sniff. Tears tracked through the dirt on her cheek, wiped quickly away.

She flat out started bawling when Alec

interjected with, "Is that really what happened?"

Caspian took in her face, roaring, "Silence, boy!"

Silence came, Wren terrified of making so much as a sniff.

And then the air trembled with a bone-deep resonance that wrapped around her like a warm blanket.

An Alpha purr.

"In exchange for the boys, you'll serve. Please me, and when I grow bored of you, you'll come home with full pockets and enough fresh water to last a year." He tapped a finger to her breastbone, leaning down so they might be eye-level. "This is the only offer I am going to make."

There was no question of if she'd say yes. Wren knew exactly what would happen to Alec and Mikael if she refused.

Eyes wet and heart hammering against her ribs, Wren accepted his offer.

It earned a victorious grin from the smug

Alpha, and an even louder purr left to jar the air.

He booped her nose. "I *will* be back tomorrow. You *will* be here, clean, dressed in something appealing, or I'll hunt down the rabid children haunting the Warrens and rip a limb off each one I find."

5

Everything had been scrubbed until her fingers were raw: floors, the door, clothing, her body, even her hair. Wren washed the day away, lost in the work so she might forget why her feet were stained brown and her home had been sent into upheaval. And between bouts of cleaning, she tended the sick boy curled up on her couch, a makeshift nest built up around him.

Two doses of costly decongestant, expired antibiotics, filtered water, compresses, and finally… *finally* he'd slept. Which is why

Caspian found her as he did, collapsed over the couch at Mikael's side. Like her boy, she was fast asleep.

A featherlight stroke on her cheek tickled enough that she slapped at the cause, groaning and pushing her face into the cushions.

A firm grip on the shoulder gave a soft shake. "Wake up, little rat. The cat's come to play."

Startled awake, Wren sucked in a quick breath, and jumped to her feet. Tugging the wrinkles from her skirt, she shook out the fabric. Her braid was grabbed next, the elastic tugged free so she might finger comb fresh waves and try to look as presentable as possible.

They had an agreement, and she was going to keep it.

Heart tattooing a panicked beat against her breast, she stood straight, trying to prove she'd followed directions. Clean, dressed in something appealing.

The Alpha was not impressed. Cocking his head, he eyeballed her nicest dress. "Where did you find that monstrosity? Whoever sold that to you did a number on moth-eaten drapes."

Looking down at the simple sundress, Wren frowned.

The sundress *was* made from old curtains… pretty ones she'd found in one of the abandoned homes sunk under the waterline. She'd rushed to grab them as water dumped in around her entry point, flooding the formerly sealed rooms. She'd chosen them over old tech she could have salvaged and sold, *that was* how much she liked them. She was proud of this dress, damnit!

For goodness sake, where did he think fabric for such things came from in the Warrens?

"Look at her cheeks getting pink. You hurt her feelings, boss."

With a shriek, Wren jumped and grasped Caspian's arm, clinging as she turned to find that two other males stood in the room. Hand to her heart, truly awake now, she looked around for the next surprise, narrowing her eyes on her sealed door, completely clueless to how the three of them had gotten in.

And then a long agitated growl escaped her when her eyes landed on the mud each of them had tracked in. Her clean floor was a wreck and an accusatory glare was leveled at the two strangers before landing upon a stone-faced Caspian.

A Caspian she immediately set free of her grip.

Disengaging, she spread the skirt he found so ugly, pointed at her chest, and mimed sewing it.

The Alpha couldn't care less.

Before he might say anything else, Wren kneeled into a crouch and set her fingers to his boot laces. If he was going to traipse around, he was not going to bring more mud with him.

Behind her, one of the strangers chuckled.

"I've seen plenty of women drop to their knees before you, sir, but never to take off your shoes."

The taller stranger, the one dressed in khakis and sporting a rather larger firearm, he was the one who spoke. She'd seen him beside Caspian in the pipeworks, remembered the tawny hair and green eyes, but didn't know who he was. Just as she didn't know the other one with the shaved head and unhinged smirk.

When she peered up at her *guest*, Wren saw him wink before saying, "He means they kneel to suck my cock."

It took her a moment to grasp his meaning. Once she had, she felt her cheeks heat, and went back to work unraveling his laces.

A hand fell to her crown, a hand that weighed heavy against her skull as it stroked. "Sweet and *raw* in her ugly dress and flowing white hair. You're not a rat at all, are you, but a little mouse all sleek and silent."

Already humiliated and growing more

nervous with each breath, Wren kept her head down and worked a boot from a large foot. The sock was surprisingly dry underneath, but she rolled it down anyway out of habit, then went to the other shoe.

He let her do this.

Just as he let her lead him to her most comfortable chair. When she went to the other men, men who had failed to follow her shoe removal lead, Caspian grumbled out a firm, "No. All of your attention today belongs to me. They're more than you can handle right now."

Turning to face Caspian, she looked any-where but at his frightening coat. Stubbled jaw marked with scars, a nose broken flat, bent and broken again. Lines by his lashes gave the impression the brute must laugh as he maimed. Mud brown eyes. Cropped brown hair. Rugged and craggy and not pretty in any way.

She mimed a cup of water, followed by tapping her lips in offering of food.

"You would share your food and drink with me?"

In answer, she stepped over the mud trail and padded barefoot to her cooking corner. Water was collected from all three dehumidifier units, poured into a purifier, and doled out into mismatched cups. Next was quick bread topped with sliced mushrooms harvested from the mud. Carried on a beloved tray she'd salvaged two years back, she marched to Caspian and let him choose which serving he might like.

He eyed the brownish water and her best food with distaste.

He hated her dress. Fine. He'd dragged mud all over her freshly cleaned floors. Okay. Her food and water were beneath a man who dressed in the skins of people…

Her tray landed on a side table with an irritated *thump*.

Snatching up a cup and a slice of mushroom topped bread, Wren set it where the boy could reach when he woke. She then took her own portion, perched on an unclaimed corner of her couch and ate.

Caspian's men found this hilarious.

She found them annoying.

And Caspian, as far as Wren was concerned, was worthy of no further hospitality.

When she swallowed the last bit of food and drained her glass, the Alpha unfurled from the chair. "Show me your nest."

Chewing her lip, she put her bare feet to the ground, a worried eye running over the sleeping Mikael.

"Kieran and Toby will keep an eye on your boy." A hand closed around her upper arm, pulling her away as Caspian grumbled, "And they will wipe up the mud on your floor."

The bald one scoffed, "With what?"

Large fingers plucked the ties at Wren's shoulders, the dress falling down before she might catch it. "With that. Burn it when you're done so I never have to see it again."

Wren tried to sign, "*Wait*," while one hand

covered her breasts and the other reached out to save her best article of clothing. A tug of war she would never win began between them, Wren fighting for her dress, hearing it rip, and already in tears.

The snarling Alpha had it from her, tossing it aside and yanking her from the room just as it landed in a puddle. She was sobbing by the time he shouldered her down the short hall past the bathing area and into the domicile's only bedroom.

The door was slammed before he gave her a rough shake. "Stop crying."

With a sniff and a shaking lip, her hands flung about a diatribe that was wasted for all he cared. Rude gestures escalated into flailing arms and more tears. Had she a voice she would have been yelling down the walls. Had she a voice she wouldn't have been in this situation in the first place.

A slap hit her cheek.

It was a bucket of cold water over the head.

Wren went still.

"Are you done?"

His callousness made her shiver, pink-tipped breasts breaking out in gooseflesh. Crossing her arms over her nipples, she glared.

"Take off your panties. I want to see what I bought."

Her hesitation encouraged Caspian's scowl. It grew meaner by the second until Wren hooked her thumbs in her underwear and shimmied them down her legs.

Peeling his vile coat from broad shoulders, the Alpha began to undress. He took his time about it, running his gaze over her body as he went.

Another Alpha had looked at her that way once, appraising, measuring her worth.

The other Alpha had not been nearly this large or dangerous.

Anger turned to terror.

Caspian's nostrils flared. He took in a

deep breath and snapped his eyes to hers. "Do you wish to nest first?"

That… was unexpected.

Wiping sweaty palms down the fronts of her thighs, Wren looked to her nest. The arrangement was pleasing for rest and safety, but not ideal for an Alpha to invade it. He would undo all her work if she didn't make room for him, so she did. Pillows were moved, fluffed, sorted and spread. Sheets were tucked, blankets arranged until it looked *right*. Until she felt comforted.

He seemed to understand the moment she'd calmed, the lightest offering of a purr softening his demand. "Invite me into it, Omega."

He was fully nude when she turned, and her eyes caught on the power of all that rippling muscle. Not a single part of the beast was soft—dipping ridges and rugged bulges —between his legs a stiffened trunk.

There had never been a gesture or signal, but Caspian lowered down and crept into the place she'd made for him. Roughened palms ran over her hips, the male moving her body until her back hit the bedding and his heft hovered over her.

"Look what I caught." He grinned, shifting so the coarse hair on his chest caught her nipples. "A little mouse. Hmm? And she's going to spread her legs for me, isn't she? Yes." Brushing his jaw against hers, he let his tongue swipe at her drying tears. "Yes, she is. My mouse is going to be a good girl."

His fingers dug into the soft flesh of her thighs, drawing them wide as Wren fought her aversion and reluctantly obeyed.

The lobe of her ear was sucked into a hot mouth. Gasping at the unexpected feeling, her eyes went wide.

This was real. An Alpha was in her nest.

His erection lay heavy on her stomach, wafting the scent of mouthwatering sweetness to tickle her nose.

"That's right, pretty mouse. Relax for me." The scratch of his unshaven beard didn't sting as she would have imagined when Caspian ran his face over her breasts. It enlivened the skin with prickles, soothed by the warmth of his breath when he began to scent her flesh.

The way his ribs expanded with each rich inhale, it made him grow so much larger. He truly was a beast pinning down a mouse, licking at her nipples until strange sounds caught in her throat.

He changed technique, the rasp of that tongue bringing an itch it failed to scratch. And he, the Alpha, grew more appreciative. The rumble in his chest called her to breathe deep of him, to allow what he willed.

To spread wider.

And somehow her legs obeyed.

The base of his cock slipped against her folds as if it had been coated in oil. It pried its way, balls heavy behind it, to tease and threaten all at once.

The breathless male growled, "My pretty mouse's tits smell of peaches and taste of cream. What, I wonder, does her cunt taste like?"

He dropped the pitch of his purr and growled.

A vibration, the buzz of anxious electricity, moved under Wren's flesh, demanding she writhe to its meter.

Hand slipping between them, Caspian replaced the pressure of his cock with that of creeping fingers.

She stiffened when he parted her labia, practically bowing off the mattress when he answered her retreat with the deepest, most licentious growl a man could produce. It came alive inside her and pushed away what made her Wren.

Head tossed back, distracted by the growing heartbeat between her legs, she answered his demanding call with a soft moan.

"Show me your eyes."

White lashes parted.

What he found there pleased him, and Caspian gave her a satisfied smile. "Who would have thought my pretty mouse would be so receptive? I've hardly touched you and your pupils are blown, slick soaking the sheets under your delicious ass." Slipping down her body, he took the fingers away until she was left wanting, uncovered in her nest and trying to sit up as if to chase after him.

"Ah, ah." The flat of a palm settled between her breasts, pushing her down against her nest. "I want my taste. I'm going to lick and suck and bite at this sweet pussy until I've drank my fill. And you will lay there like a good little girl and bear it."

When his eyes tracked from her face, over her spit-shined breasts to land between her legs, the magic was lost.

Another Alpha had pulled her pussy lips apart once, leaning close to inspect and confirm. He'd declared her a virgin before taking her off to the room with a couch.

Caspian's hand on her chest kept her pinned when the appeal of Alpha purr failed. Try as she might, she couldn't close her legs no matter how her muscles trembled with effort so long as the male held them open.

She couldn't stop the shamed flush and panicked noises that squeaked past her throat.

Nor could she repress the full body shudder that bent her spine when a fat tongue rasped delicate flesh from anus to mound.

"Delicious, but naughty." He spoke as he tongued her, as he lapped and sucked and destroyed all reason. "Bad girl! I told you not to move." He took a nip at her clit, chuckling when she yelped. "Bad girls get fucked, good girls get played with. Are you trying to tell me you want to get fucked already?"

How could anyone be still when nerves caught fire?

The vibration of his laughter and another of those terrible growls set her wheeling into a place of sensation that stole all sense. He piled more on top of it, flicking her clit with the tip of his tongue until she uncontrollably bucked against his mouth.

Something breached her, something thick

and wriggling. It hooked behind her pubic bone and pulled until she screamed. In and out it pumped while flick, flick, flick, went that tongue.

A river seeped from her pussy.

"Mmmmmmhhrrmm." The only sound she could make. Louder and louder it built, just as the tension curled in on itself like an imploding star.

This was how she was going to die. Her legs spread, mashing her pussy into the face of a killer.

Light broke inside her when the male grew rough. She shined, more slick flowed, all of it sucked up in slurps by a rampaging tongue.

"Only. Good. Girls." The swirl and dance of his tongue staccatoed her clit between words. "Get. To. Cum."

Insides locked on the writhing digit rubbing inside her pussy, they seized like a vise —sucking upward, milking Caspian's fingers for a substance they could never provide. The resulting orgasm was indescribable. It tore away everything, left her truly *raw* and shaken to her hungry dissatisfied core.

But it had pleased the fuck out of the man who had forced it on her.

Grinning, as he licked his lips and met her eyes, Caspian climbed over her spent body and growled, "Brace yourself, mouse. You're about to get fucked like the bad, bad girl you are."

6

Virgin pussy tasted sweeter than goddamn wine.

Another Alpha might have bought the mouse and forced in his knot, but no one else had tasted her or fucked her proper. The Beta-drunk Alphas who thought they ran this city hardly even knew where to stick it. They got their rocks off easy and often with their stables of Betas, buying Omegas only for bragging rights and to breed.

It wasn't the first time Caspian had heard of a girl being cast off for failing to come after a few quick thrusts and hard cuff to the face. Most Omegas squeezed in their panic, clenching hard enough around a knot for an Alpha to spurt a load. The privileged males couldn't tell the difference in sensation and had no idea what they were missing.

They didn't know how to tease an Omega into bloom or know how to make a mute one sing.

Caspian might not have been handsome like Kieran, or charismatic like Toby, but he was perceptive in a way most people couldn't imagine. He knew what the mouse needed and gave it so he could take all *he* wanted and more.

It was utterly selfish and completely delightful.

To see her sprawled sweaty and slick-covered under him, to watch astounded lavender eyes turn black with lust—his cock ached as it pulsated in his fist.

Her nest would be in ruins by the time he was done. He'd paint the walls of her hovel in cum and walk away smiling, knowing she'd never get the smell out.

Her pink little pussy still fluttered against him, soft rolls of her hips spreading him with all that slippery invitation. Snowy-white skin, head pillowed in soft wisps of hair, puffed pink nipples and a soft smile under lust-drunk eyes. Pretty as a picture, and he couldn't wait to watch her face screw up in pleasure as he pumped her full of thick ropes of sticky Alpha sperm.

The thought alone and he spurt just enough precum to splash her belly and startle the little thing out of her swoon. Good. He wanted her lucid when he tore into that hole, wanted to see the play of pain and pleasure ripple across her face.

Cockhead swollen red, Caspian leaned over her and jerked off until another spurt hit her perfect tits. Fuuuuck, it looked pretty there. Sweet as honey on a strawberry.

Dipping his head to swipe up a glob, he moved to her lips and spit it right on her tongue. Her little choke and successive following hum left him satisfied. She liked his taste as much as he liked hers, which was good, because he was going to cum down that throat until sperm leaked from her eyeballs.

Skull fucking that mouth while Toby fucked her ass and Kieran destroyed her pussy…

Caspian spurt again, catching the sweet stuff in his palm. Again he licked it up and brought it to her parted lips, jamming his tongue deep to coat her palate with his flavor.

He wondered how she'd look with a woman feasting between her legs, if she'd hate it and silently beg him to stop her. He almost hoped so. She'd come so fucking flawlessly despite her disgust, eyes locked on his, cheeks flushed from pleasure and shame.

"Fuck…" Breathless and rattling out a growl demanding submission, Caspian put a stop to the fantasies and looked reality right in her blown eyes.

Mushroom tip notched where the mouth

of her cunt suckled with each squirm, he found her resistant when his hips tilted.

Tight and ready to be subjugated.

An inch was gained, Caspian grinding his teeth and straining with the ferocity of his growl.

The call set her still, but left her cunt fluttering only enough that a rough jolt forward buried merely half his length in spasming perfection.

Shouting, he pulled out a fraction of the way and reared back until she squealed. "My little mouse is going to take all this cock and choke her cunt on it!"

The muscles in his ass clenched tight, he drove forward again and fought his way through the last of her body's resistance. The Omega began to shiver beneath him, somewhat in shock and somewhat in desire, but he was too far gone to notice.

The rut came full upon him, the Alpha mindless in his quest to seed fertile ground. Cunt walls slippery with slick, clenched and rattled as he pounded his dick deeper yet. The wet sucking sound of her pussy, the smack of his balls against her ass, each note stabbed into the base of his cock swelling it bigger and bigger.

He sucked the tip of one bobbing tit so hard the female shrilled. He moved to the other breast to bite and bruise so she'd know who'd fucked her. All the while, paltry scratches from petite hands brought a pleasing sting to his back and arms.

Her body was ready; he could smell it in the tinge of her fear.

Knot throbbing with renewed vigor to engorge, he ground her down into that sad nest and hooked the sweet spot behind her pelvis.

His every throb would tease that bundle of nerves, edging her closer to true bloom and his own ultimate release.

"Fight all you want, pretty mouse. There's no getting away now." No chance of escape. All she could do was surrender to a greater power.

Sucking a kiss from a hissing mouth, Caspian stole a thumb between their warring pelvises to rub careful circles on the sweet little clit he'd excited into a pert nub. His balls drew painfully tight when she jolted at one touch, boiling seed churning into that which would be a mighty first eruption.

"I'm going to fill you up with so much cum, it will be leaking down your thighs for a week—bloat out that little belly, you'll be so full." Violently rocking against her, rubbing his knot in the spot that would make her wail, he watched blown eyes roll back in her skull.

Faster his thumb went until the Omega made the perfect soundless scream.

The clench around his knot twisted like a pair of hands, streaming up his aching shaft to pull the cum right out of his balls. He flooded her with globs of jizz, glorying in her whines for mercy.

The little mouse reared back, legs kicking out in an attempt to unseat him.

Fierce for something so small.

Beautiful in her mindless surrender to orgasm.

A second great volley of seed shot past the knot to spray out the head of his cock, an Alpha roar shaking the walls.

She drew out a third, a fourth, and a fifth burst of pleasure, milking him for all she was worth until Caspian was sure his balls had shriveled to nothing.

"Good girl."

Bad, bad, dirty, naughty girl. He was going to do such *things* to her.

A whine on the end of her every breath, his captured mouse's internal wrench began to ebb. The knot bobbed in time to the beat of his heart, trapping all he'd spilled and leaving Caspian thoroughly satisfied.

He hadn't come that hard in… maybe ever… and the greedy male was in no hurry to give it up. Wet, hot heat would stay wrapped around him for an hour yet if he was any judge.

Already tempted to wring another orgasm

out of her just so he could make her clench around his impressive knot, Caspian licked at her neck. A purr rattled from him louder than any he'd offered a good fuck in the past, one that put his little captive straight into a stupor.

Free to move her as he wished, he sat back on his heels, drawing her little body with him. With her draped down his thighs he got a good view of her pussy stuffed with his meat. Glorious. That was a stretch she'd feel for days to come, each twinge when she walked reminding her of who owned her now.

Her pretty clit was trying to hide under its hood. Caspian peeled back the skin and gave the shiny nub a light flick. His Omega twitched but didn't wake.

"Kieran." Caspian didn't need to turn to know his pack mate stood behind him. He'd smelled him from the moment he'd stepped into the room.

Chuckling, arousal in his voice, his subordinate said, "I hope you don't mind that I took in the end of the show? With all that noise, I came in thinking I'd have to stop you from claiming the girl."

"Come here." Voice hoarse and breathless, Caspian waved off the idea as if he hadn't been extremely tempted to bite down on soft skin. "Suck her. I need to feel her come again."

His Second-Alpha didn't need to be told twice. Stomping right through the nest, Kieran went to his knees at his boss' side and buried his face where Caspian held back the hood from the Omega's tender clit.

Though he couldn't see more than the back of his Second's head, Caspian could feel the warm spit and swipe of another man's tongue when it brushed his shaft as he pleasured the mouse.

Dazed, she began to arch and buck, still locked tight to a pulsating knot.

Watching for the moment, she realized another partook of her body, Caspian began to rock his shaft inside her again.

Just as she began to peak, her eyes flew open, a ring of violet around huge pupils.

High as a fucking kite on him and already eager to climax again.

Without lifting his head from her nub, Kieran reached out a hand and covered her scream. The girl came even harder than the first time, wringing more sperm from Caspian's cock until he was certain he was bone dry. And still she came and came until tears ran from the corner of her eyes and Caspian had to rip Kieran off.

His Second wiped the back of his hand over his slick-smeared mouth, eyes wild with need as he growled, "I want to fuck her next."

"No." Not yet. The little mouse only just had her first taste of what was to come. "You can have Rosie tonight. I'm done with her."

Watching the distraught Omega, Kieran offered the purr Caspian was unable to create, still groaning in pleasure as he was.

The Second-Alpha's hand brushed sweat-soaked hair from the woman, admiring what they both knew was a special kind of beauty. "When can I have this one? I want to know what made you roar like that."

Barely able to catch his breath, little spurts still being drawn from his near empty sack, Caspian gave a lopsided grin. "Fuck Rosie. I'm not ready to share."

"And Toby?"

"Have him take that boy to a doctor." All this fun would go to shit if that kid died before Caspian was done with his new toy. "When he's back, he can fuck Rosie too."

7

———

Wren would never forget the sensation of a cork popping—hot fluid spraying out between her legs, irritating stinging skin and leaving a lapping puddle under the blanket.

She'd still been in a daze when that fat snake of meat had slithered from her body, the stroke of a rough-skinned hand down the side of her face Caspian's only goodbye.

She'd slept like the dead when it was done, waking sore and sticky…

And lonesome.

The sound of the boys' gaming console blared its racket in the front room, encouraging Wren to forget her embarrassment and climb groaning from the soiled nest. Hand pressed between her legs, fingers growing drenched with the lingering taint that dripped out, she limped to her dresser and dug out some clothes.

Soft flannel seemed to scratch such sensitive skin, pants leaving her hissing in pain when pulled them over bruises.

She felt filthy both in body and spirit, biting back a cry when she turned and saw the state of her nest.

Wreckage.

Unwilling to wade through cum-soaked bedding to fix it, Wren turned her back and went to the door.

Forcing herself forward, she breathed through the aching discomfort between her legs and rounded the hall to find it was not

Mikael slapping the controller and cursing at the screen.

He saw her the second she saw him—the shaved head Alpha who'd broken into her home with his boss.

The entirety of his carriage changed when she instinctively snarled, the male no longer casual or focused on fun. He moved slowly, lowering the controller and rising to stand. "I'm Toby."

Who cared?

The couch had no Mikael on it. Where was her boy?

"There are books in here, so Caspian assumed you knew how to read." The voice didn't match the gruff demeanor or creepy smirk. It was cultured, educated even. The man gestured to the coffee table where his feet had rested only moments before. "He left you a letter."

That would mean she had to walk closer to this stranger, and that was the last thing she wanted to do.

"Can you read?"

In a temper, Wren signed, *"Read this, you fucking scumbag. Where is Mikael?"*

"I picked up the read part and the fuck bit. I think it's safe to say the rest was something you're going to regret later."

"I regret every goddamn thing that happened today!"

"Calm down. I'm not here to upset you." The man held his hands out in a conciliatory gesture, but failed to lose that unsettling grin or the unwavering stare. "You got a raw deal. Have a seat, I'll get you some water. You'll read the letter, and that will be that."

The need to know her boy was okay outweighed her need to stay away from all males forever. Hobbling cautiously closer, Wren snatched the folded paper, backing away as soon as it was in her fingers. When her back hit the wall, she set her eyes to the chicken scratch:

The boy was taken to a doctor in the Shirley District.

-C

Tossing the letter aside she signed, *"Which doctor? I want to see him! Where is Alec?"*

"I don't know what you're saying." But he damn well knew what her intent was.

The boys. The reason she pressed a hand between her aching legs and slipped down to the floor until her butt hit cracked tile. They were her reason for all of it and neither of them were here.

Alec had not come home. Mikael was sick… and now missing.

And she had whored herself out...

Taking a second to regroup, to figure out why the room was spinning, Wren closed her eyes and tried to think.

Toby trod across the tile to use her filtration system and pour a fresh cup. When he reached where she'd tucked her head against her knees, he patted her shoulder, murmuring, "Here. You're lightheaded because you need water. Lots of water. Omegas are special in this way."

She took the cup expressly so he'd back away, which he did. And then she drank. When it was empty he gave her another.

"I have something for you. It might cheer you up."

Rubbing her temples, Wren hardly spared him a look. Still, his smirk became a full-fledged grin.

Reaching behind her couch, he pulled pretty fabric out with a flourish. Her dress.

Her favorite dress.

Pathetic, she stared at it, eyes wet and heart giving a single thump.

He crept forward, dress in hand, until he kneeled where she sat. "Keep it. Caspian doesn't need to know."

Tentative fingers stretched out to touch the coarse weave.

Snatching it to her nose, Wren buried her face in something familiar and special, breathing in lungfuls of air that smelled how she had before an Alpha drenched her in his filth.

"Come on." Careful of the bruises on her arm, he pulled her up. "Let's get you back to bed."

Dress clutched to her chest, she stumbled beside him, the place between her legs throbbing. He bore more of her weight than she was willing to admit, going so far as to wrap an arm around her waist. Once back in her room, the ruined nest gave her no comfort. So Wren pushed free of her guide, grabbing a pillow and the only dry blanket in the puddle of cum. Both were dragged to the corner where she plopped down and fell asleep almost instantly.

When morning came, she was shivering in the corner alone without the sound of either boy banging around in the front room.

In misery.

MANAGING REPAIRS ON THE PIPEWORKS, keeping rival factions from gaining even an inch of his hard-won labors, and negotiating with the thirsty powers-that-be tended to keep a man busy, but still Caspian found himself regularly checking the camera feeds recording the Omega's hovel.

Toby had done well with the install; the tiny surveillance machines buried into the crumbling brick had gone unnoticed. Every single room, all angles, were available. Not that he'd needed to access more than two so far.

His Omega had not left the corner of her room in three days except to hobble to the bathroom or to grab more of that bracken she called water.

She had not taken any food. Not even the shit fungus she'd tried to offer him when he'd come to call.

It was starting to piss him off.

He controlled ninety-percent of the water

supply to the entirety of Dale City. Everyone who knew his name knew not to fuck with him.

If the pretender Alpha government lording over them from above wanted clean drink, they had to pay. If they failed to pay, he shut off the valves and let the thirsty snobs above sort out new management. It never took long. After all, a human would die without water in a handful of days.

Racketeering was good, honest money.

Caspian had every Alpha in a thousand-mile radius by the balls.

And still that Omega pouted in the corner, clinging to her torn dress Toby had disregarded orders to save for her.

He had fucked her a bit more roughly than he'd intended too, sure. She *had* fought back in spectacular fashion… but she had also come gloriously multiple times.

What was the issue?

Why had she not repaired her nest or obsessively cleaned? He could still see mud smudges on the floor in the front room. Why had she not come to him?

By this point, the Omega should have been scratching at his door asking for trinkets, credits… affection.

Fuck, Rosie had been begging for his cock after the very first poke. Now that he had set her aside, she was skulking around trying to entice him back. He never went back to an old meal for more than a passing fuck, but he wasn't a total bastard either. The women were allowed to stay under his protection if they wanted to. They were given comforts, food, and clean water. But they also had to serve for the privilege of belonging.

Rosie was exclusively for Toby and Kieran's enjoyment now. When his Second and Third were done with her, the general population would fight over that gnawed bone.

Someday the little mouse would face that too.

Or she'd scuttle back to her hovel a little richer in both credits and experience. Which might be for the best.

Caspian didn't enjoy the image of her catering to his workers, at least not until he'd supped his fill. For now, she was his. And until defensive instincts ran their course, he wasn't going to share… unless it was for his own pleasure.

The mouse would be lovely, pale and perfect, mauled by his Kieran and Toby.

Eventually. But not yet.

Not until Caspian had gorged.

"Your cock is dripping down the front of your pants, boss." Fucking Toby had been enjoying his distraction with the surveillance feeds a bit too much.

Adjusting what had become a never-ending erection, Caspian gave a sincerely vicious warning growl to back off. "Unless you're planning to suck me off, get the fuck away from me."

His Third chuckled. "Never seen you in *the rut* before. Why not have sweetcheeks brought here and take what's yours until it passes?"

Because something about having that Omega exposed to any of this felt extremely wrong.

Toby looked at the screen where a curled up mouse slept in the corner. "A lot of pride for one little girl. She hasn't even tried to fix that sorry excuse for a nest."

The rejection stung, and Caspian was growing livid. She should have been lying in his scent, crawling to his door, begging him for scraps!

He was going to go over there and fuck her until she knew who owned her. Until every inch of her skin was marked with his cum and bleeding from bites.

No… not bites. Powerful Alphas never claimed a single Omega. That was for the weak. Men like him bred them all, fucked who they would.

Omegas were only a commodity to be traded and shared.

Toby mocked in a whisper as he walked past, "Take her something pretty. Maybe she'll forgive you for ruining her favorite dress."

8

———————

It was so quiet without the boys running in and out. Alec wasn't coming back anytime soon; not until his temper was spent. Wren had come to terms with that, but she hated having ten-year-old Mikael gone.

She hated that not one knock had come to her door. No one wanted her wares now that the rumor must have spread that Caspian had come to call.

How was she to salvage this?

A person couldn't exactly start over in the Warrens. This was it, there was nowhere to go. And she couldn't afford passage to a higher neighborhood, not for all the kids and herself. And even if she could, there would be little honest work for a woman marked *Defective*.

How would she feed them?

All valuable salvage was hidden under the sinking, mud-spattered Warrens.

Pointing her toes, flexing them, and pointing them again, Wren counted the cracks in the wall.

This home wouldn't last much longer. It would sink in a year, two tops. Already it was dangerously close to the waterline. A single tremor and she'd be drowned.

The boys deserved better.

In order to provide it, Wren had to get off the floor.

But everything ached; her mouth was cotton, and her eyes could not be trusted. She kept seeing men in her room. First the shaved head invader who'd given her back the dress tucking a scratchy blanket around her. Then the shaggy haired gunman pressing water to her lips.

And now… now it almost looked as if Caspian stood in her door.

"You haven't eaten in three days."

A slow blink and Wren closed her eyes.

"You have not repaired your nest."

That thing was no longer a nest. It was a cesspool where she'd been used and abandoned. Not fit for rats… or even a *mouse.*

"Don't you want to know how Mikael is doing?"

This dream was cruel, cruel enough to trick her into opening her eyes again.

The phantom Alpha had come even closer. "I have brought you food."

She wasn't hungry.

"And clean water."

The water she provided was fine.

The ground grew lumpy as if the foundations were already bursting apart. Soon the mud would rush in and she'd be buried like the kids outside.

Except she didn't sink down, she rose up.

Thumping against warmth, the frost infecting her limbs began to sting.

"You shouldn't have left me alone," her eyes said when they met muted brown. *"You wrecked everything I built."*

A warm cheek in need of a shave scrubbed hers. "Even when I'm angry with you, I can't help but think that you're a sweet little mouse."

Her nostrils filled with a spice that perked up her lungs and set her stomach twisting.

Gruff, warm and male, the voice at her ear promised, "If you keep looking at me like that, I won't feed you first…"

The idea of food sounded lovely. Minced mushrooms on sour bread. Maybe a juicy hunk of opossum.

That was not what a fat finger poking between her lips set upon her tongue once he'd sat.

It was something familiar and heady, seasoned with salt and some kind of herb. Meat that squished without bone fragments or gristle when chewed.

Heavenly.

So damn good that, in her haze, she latched onto the finger that offered savory reward and sucked every last drop of juice away. When the flavor went from meat to man, she spit out the digit and launched her own attack on the carcass nestled in a plastic sack on her coffee table.

Chicken.

God, she had forgotten what it tasted like, gobbling down this impossible dream without thought for manners or consideration for the purring beast who braced her on his lap. Finger in her mouth, licking the juice from her palms, Wren hardly drew breath between swallows—only pausing long enough to wrap her greasy hands around the glass of clear water set nearby.

She ate until it hurt, and then she ate some more.

She gorged until she realized this wasn't a

dream, and lacked the will to care that an awful man would mock her for this later.

She cleaned that whole damn chicken, panting at the boney aftermath as if she were offended it had run out of meat.

And then she began to suck the marrow.

And he let her.

He let her lick and gnaw. Let her stoop over the meal as if she were ready to fight to the death for it. All the while rubbing her back in slow circles.

He even reached past her carnage to lift up a cistern and refill the grease-smeared glass. "Drink more."

Wren didn't do it because he'd ordered her. She did it because she was so fucking thirsty and water was hard to come by. The way she slammed the empty cup down on the pockmarked wood said that loud and clear.

Again it was refilled.

But she couldn't hold another drop.

"Mouse." A nose nestled into her tangled

hair, large hands slipping where they would. "I'm angry with you."

Too full by half to be anything but satisfied, Wren let him touch and sniff.

"I looked in your storage. There wasn't any food."

Yeah… only rich people stored food. Warrens rats fought to find it daily and most of them didn't have to feed two growing boys.

"And your water is shit—distilled until there are no minerals left and hardly wiped of rust from your garbage machines."

Well, fuck you too.

Glancing over her shoulder, Wren looked the purring male in the eye. He didn't look angry at all. In fact, he looked extremely content to sit on her couch and keep her settled over his thigh.

Simple signs said, *"I do my best."*

Though he could not have understood, he nodded. "Of course you do."

Well, that was…

Her brief moment of respite drained down

to her toes. He hadn't come here to spoil her with food and share his water. He'd come here for sex.

He, the man who knew where Mikael was.

And they had a deal.

Reaching for the hem of her dirty shirt, she lifted it up so they might get it over with. Breasts bouncing free, hair disheveled, she pulled it off and faced him.

Mud brown eyes went to pink nipples, a darting tongue wetting Caspian's lips. "Kiss my neck and tell me that you're grateful. Show me that you want me."

What Wren wanted was to curl up into a ball, digest all this food, and rest. But she obeyed and pressed her exposed breasts to his clothing-covered chest until dry lips met male skin.

She couldn't find it in her to kiss him. It wasn't willfulness, it was…

It was sadness.

He'd asked for a kiss. Wren chose instead

to wrap her arm around his neck and embrace the enemy. Cooing and shushing as she would have one of her boys, she nestled. Careful fingertips danced over the tense muscles of Caspian's neck, then dipped under that disgusting coat and kneaded tension away.

She gave him a feast of everything but lust. True attention. Generosity of spirit.

And when his head rolled back against the sagging cushions of her couch, Wren gave him a purr.

9

____

Caspian hardly recognized the rumbling contentment humming in his chest. It wasn't a purr offered to manipulate and calm an Omega, it was the sound of unadulterated male gratification.

The little mouse had lulled him out of the rut and right into a doze.

And she had kept him in that state by curling up on his lap and finding her own rest. She snored, a little whirring female purr. It was extremely cute.

Soft and pliable and filled with food he'd given her.

His cock stirred, a twitch of pulsing blood engorging tingling flesh. He wanted to be inside her while she made that noise, to feel her touch him as she did before she'd closed her eyes to catnap.

Women didn't touch men like that. Not men like him.

Once or twice Caspian had caught Rosie rubbing against Kieran when she didn't know her owner could see. It was the handsome ones who earned enticing touches. Scarred up men like him had to fuck bitches first to show them what they were missing.

And then sluts spread with enthusiasm for what he could offer, groveling at his feet in a bid for rank.

For the last six months, Rosie had saved all her best tricks for *his* cock. She'd whispered sweet words and praised him because he was First-ranked Alpha—because *he* was kingpin—but she would never have played like his mouse.

There would have been no gentleness on a couch. After her meal, Rosie would have swallowed his cock, bobbing up and down as she'd slathered him with stringy spit. She would have fucked him in whatever vile way she thought he might like best.

Done *anything*.

The mouse hadn't even thought to stroke his dick. She had given pleasure in other ways, while taking comfort of her own. The sour anxiety in her scent had faded into sweet sleepiness. She had even willingly put her ear to his heart just to listen.

He should not have left a female like her alone for three days after breaking her in.

The sleek, raw mouse *needed* more than just a meal. She'd needed an Alpha. Otherwise she'd end up like Rosie, vying for attention in a bid to secure rank amongst the kept females.

"Sir, you're needed back at the pipeworks." Since his arrival, Kieran had been watching them as if unsure what to make of the scene. His Second was perplexed, those green eyes women preened for locked on Caspian's Omega.

A masculine rumble thick with content-ment said, "It can wait."

Kieran eased closer, leaning forward to sniff the female. "What is she doing?"

Was that a hint of jealousy in his Second's tone? Caspian's dick grew all the harder, the soft bottom butting up against it wiggling in unconscious response. "She's earning another good meal, if nothing else. I'm almost tempted to…"

"To what?" Piercing green eyes darted from the sleeping mouse's face to meet his, Kieran cocking a brow. "Are you… are you smiling?"

"I want you to watch me fuck her." Why did that feel so good to say, and not just in the carnal sense? Caspian wanted the Second to sit and wait, and watch a woman who had purred only for him come apart.

"Can I touch her?"

An instant refusal came to his tongue, bitten back before it was more than a growl. His Second and Third had every right to demand their share, but for once, Caspian was not eager to offer. "Afterward."

A trace of challenge, a reminder of what they were, led Kieran to narrow his eyes. "Toby will expect to at least lick her clean."

That was an action beneath First Alpha and even *that* was more than Caspian wanted to share. Agitation hooked into the slipping sense of calm, leaving his stone-hard dick instantly uncomfortable. "Summon him when you are ready and I'll leave you to it. See that he remembers his place."

A handsome grin bloomed, Kieran chuckling. "Still pissed he gave her back that dress?"

Caspian had watched the recorded feed and

seen how she'd clung to it for days. Even now, it was moldering in the corner of her bedroom. As punishment, Toby had been pinned and dominated. He had been splashed with his First's seed and made to swallow. "He had his orders."

"You know how he gets with women."

Grave, Caspian drove the point home. "I know he's killed three of the whores in my pen."

Kieran shrugged as if their loss was nothing. "Betas."

"She will see him on his best behavior. Do you understand me?" Caspian reached out, collaring his Second-Alpha in a menacing grip.

The second most dangerous Alpha in Dale City complied without question. "Yes, sir."

Kieran's throat was set free, Caspian running a touch over a milky white arm instead. The fine hairs under his fingertips rose, the mouse stirring. Lavender eyes blinked open just in time for the Omega to hear, "The mouse will rebuild her nest today. Praise her when it's finished."

"And if she disobeys?"

"Rape her."

The Omega's sweet purr dried up, the air once again soured with anxiety.

Pinching her chin, gentle as a monster might be, Caspian said, "Come now, sweet mouse. You'll be a good girl for Kieran and Toby, so there is no reason to be afraid. But should my mouse choose to turn into an ordinary rat, she will be treated like one. Understood?"

The girl nodded, swallowing.

He booped her nose. "Feeling better?"

She nodded again, slower as if unsure what he expected.

"I've enjoyed the view of your tits for the last two hours, but it's your cunt I want to see now. Strip. Stand with your legs apart in front of me and pull your pussy open."

Lavender eyes darted to the other male, but not in eager anticipation. Her body language made it very clear she didn't want the Second-Alpha anywhere near this.

Shy…

A fierce sense of triumph roiled in Caspian's stomach. His mouse wasn't hoping the pretty boy would play, and it excited him. Stern and hungry for his due, he warned, "He's already tasted your pussy, pretty mouse. And he will again if I order it. Get up and obey me. Spread those cunt lips and let me see."

Climbing from his lap, she peeled her lower layers away. With a deep breath, she faced him full on, legs spread wide, her fingers caught on the sweet outer lips until the ripe inner flesh was on display.

Caspian reached forward, tracing a finger over all he found. Light stimulation, perhaps even the humiliation, brought drops of dew to collect at her opening, easing the slip of his exploration when he thrust two fingers as deep as he could reach.

A twist and a whirl and he pulled them

free, holding shiny digits up for inspection. "I don't see any blood. Did that hurt?"

The flash of temptation to lie leapt into her gaze and just as quickly vanished. She shook her head no.

"You're healed enough for what I have in mind." His hand went to his belt, working the leather and the zipper until his pants gaped open and his cock sprang free. If she was surprised by the display in front of the other male, the mouse kept it off her face. Though she did twitch when Kieran settled on the couch beside him, the Second reaching down to free his own growing erection.

"I want him to see how sweet you are to me." Male hands cupped her hips, Caspian drawing her forward to straddle his lap. "You are going to be a good little mouse and ride my cock."

Beside them, Kieran pulled at his dick, knee braced so he might see every lovely swell and dip of the girl about to be used.

When lavender eyes went wide, Caspian

caught her chin and brought her back under his spell. "Good girls keep their eyes on mine, hmmm? Kieran only gets to watch your body. I'm not in the mood to share your attention."

Between them, Caspian stroked his girth, moving in time with his Second until a little well of precum glistened at his tip. There was a subtle shift to her hips once the scent of his offering tickled her nose. Unknowingly, she presented.

Kieran choked up harder on his dick. "If you don't growl, I'm going to. I need to see that cunt flood."

In a rare concession to a subordinate's desire, Caspian began a low extended rumbling. That first spurt from her slit doused his cockhead, slick dripping over his jerking fingers like hot fudge on a sundae. Warm and slippery, it sweetened the air.

His Second groaned, leaning close, hand jerking his shaft. He began to sniff and lick his lips, to growl under his breath… to almost whine. "Fuuuuuck."

Sluicing his cockhead in the slippery mess still dripping from the mouse, Caspian grunted. "Eyes on me, princess. Eyes only on me."

The lavender burned with just enough anxiety to slow the encroaching pupil, yet her desire bloomed nonetheless.

Swallowing as if already gripped by her cunt, he ordered, "Use your hands on me how you did before."

It took a moment for the mouse to grasp his intent, but then those hands slipped under his coat. He watched her as she learned the shape of his body, explored his superior strength—her cunt dripping out the perfect substance to keep the fist jerking his cock well-lubricated.

"Purr and make your little noises." The second she did, he groaned like an untried boy, spurting another wave of precum to splash against her pussy and edging her body even further into need.

At his side, Kieran slowed his pace, the

man already fighting back the threat of a knot at the base of his cock. Her smell was just that fucking good.

Knowing his Second suffered just as much, as he relished this moment, Caspian took the little mouse in hand. Lined up with that sweet hole, he drew her down until she grimaced and began to push up.

"I didn't tell you to stop." Bruising her hips with his grip, he hissed, "Slide down my cock like a good girl, or I'll shove it into you the way I punish a bad girl."

Pained noises caught in her throat. She breathed in shallow pants and let gravity impale her on his rod. Ass met his thighs, her lip shaking, but wisely she never closed her eyes in pain.

She'd held his gaze just as he'd ordered, and would be rewarded for it.

He growled again, smirking as he kneaded her hips. In response, her insides marginally loosened, reducing her discomfort and encouraging more slick.

A symphony of confusion and desire burned in her expression, little twinges of pain and beautiful shocks of pleasure inspired and extended at Caspian's leisure.

Cock throbbing in her internal grip, balls already starting to swell in anticipation of a glorious eruption, he drew his mouse closer for a kiss.

Even with his tongue in her mouth, she kept her eyes open, she kept them locked on his as if nothing else in the world existed.

"Fuck me?" Had he just asked her? Was that pleading in his voice?

There wasn't time to decide, not when an infinitely distracting cunt squeezed where he ached and drew up a shaft desperate for friction. Caspian showed her how to move, guiding her hips as he breathed in her air. Once she had the measure of it, his hands wandered of their own volition— arms threading around her back until one tangled in the hair at the base of her skull and the other hooked her closer.

Why had he not ordered her to remove his clothing first? How could he have thought a simple fuck on her disgusting couch would be enough?

Those abnormally white tits should have been slipping over his bared chest, not pressed to his shirt instead. He should have felt her hair trailing over his arms. The skins of his slaughtered enemies wasn't worthy to brush against her flesh.

"Ride me faster, circle your hips. Gah..." He choked, gasping when her pussy gave a lurch and slammed down just as he desired. "Jesus, mouse. Take what you want!"

Her hands fisted in his shirt, she bucked, chasing after what drove her. Her need for *his* cum.

Going to town wringing his own meat, Kieran's eyes were glued to where the mouse's pussy swallowed and spit out an angry, red Alpha cock. He was chiming with them a steady, "Yes, yes, just like that. Fuck him as hard as you can."

Eyes black as Caspian's heart, completely high on his call, the mouse did. She *fucked* him.

He just sat back and took it.

The sounds she made would have made an old sailor blush, the squelch and suck of a dripping cunt seasoning the air and driving both Alphas wild.

Slapping down hard on Caspian's thighs, her body called for the knot, his skin bursting to deliver what she craved. He swelled so hot and so fast that she was caught, the Omega past reason as she squealed and began to lurch. Whatever was happening inside her was heaven on his cock, the rippling suck of her orgasm fierce and violent.

Mouth parted, unblinking eyes stared straight through him. He gave her three massive gushes in such rapid succession he grew lightheaded.

Her greedy pussy demanded more, biting down with such fervor on his knot that he clawed for her throat in response.

"Careful, Caspian!"

Another wave of lava rushed from aching balls, up a pulsating shaft to spray from the slit in his cockhead and batter her insides with foamy seed. Another and another until he was whining with each breath, so far twisted up in pleasure, he couldn't remember his name.

When he was certain his cock would split like an over-cooked sausage, the squeezing ripple let up. The following wave of euphoria was stronger than any drug he sold on the streets.

In his grip, a pale throat had gone pink, above it bug-eyed and gasping for air, the mouse rode the cusp of a blackout. Stranger still was the unwelcome male who had him by the hair and braced his weight between Caspian's snapping teeth and the floundering girl's shoulder.

"Once you claim her there's no going back!"

Sense cracked through exuberant lust, and Caspian threw her neck from his grip without consideration for how they were joined. She rocked back, arms wheeling, caught by his Second, who still braced a hand against Caspian's chest as if expecting the First-Alpha to make another grab for her.

As her vision began to clear and huge gasping sucks of air finally made their way into her ribcage, the Omega began to wail. These were the kind of sobs threats and a strong backhand would not crush. She was beyond consoling, completely terrified, and retching up stringy mucus past a damaged throat.

Caspian had never felt a knot retreat so quickly. The wave of cum that splattered his pants when he shifted her off should have given him great pride. Hell, it was more than he'd ever dumped in a female in all his myriad liaisons. Even Rosie with all her tricks had had never drawn forth half so much.

Standing abruptly, fixing up his fly, Caspian looked down at the mess he'd cre-ated. The little mouse cowered. "You're not defective." When she failed to raise up her face and acknowledge that she'd heard him, he tried to mollify again, "You're flawless. Best fuck I've ever had."

The petrified thing shrunk further in on herself.

Resting a hand on her head, he fought past his own sense of shock and struggled to create a purr. Offering the closest thing to an apology she was ever going to get, Caspian said, "It wasn't intentional. You didn't do anything wrong."

She stilled under his stroking hand, but it was out of fright, not calm. Unsure how to handle her, Caspian backed up a step. The effect on the Omega was immediate.

She wanted him gone.

"Supply whatever she needs: food, water, new bedding for the nest. If a doctor is required, one will be brought here."

"Sir?" His Second stood there baffled and did nothing.

Roaring his displeasure, Caspian snarled, "Fucking comfort her already!"

A second later he was slamming her door shut at his back, face a mask of outright violence.

10

———————

Wren's mind and body had yet to fully reconnect. Parts of her were twitching mercilessly, firing off residual bursts of muscle cramping pleasure, yet ferocious pain circled her neck and her lungs burned with each breath.

Gasping for air, Wren sobbed.

The Alpha had almost murdered her the moment her body had found an earth shattering completion of spirit. His violence had skyrocketed her elation. The way he'd snapped his teeth hadn't frightened her at all.

She'd fed on his frenzy and orgasmed all the harder.

Throat a pulped mush, Wren couldn't help but wish he'd killed her.

She couldn't live like this.

"Shhhh, Omega." The one called Kieran stroked her naked spine, his purr gaining strength with each passing minute.

She'd willingly, even enthusiastically, ridden an evil man's cock, while striking green eyes bore witness…

Kieran had taken pleasure in what he'd seen.

Still took pleasure even now if the jutting member between his legs was any indication. It dripped scented fluid, adding to the pool of semen and slick that still spilled from her pussy to smear the floor under her bruised knees.

The longer he lingered and pathetically tried to console, the more his motivation for doing so became apparent.

Once or twice, the hand exploring the

curve of her bent spine had slipped over rounded ass cheeks to trail where sensitive flesh still tingled. Though she'd shied, he'd found what he sought, bringing drenched fingers to his mouth. After, a quick suck and a snarled warning when Wren tried to back away, self-preservation kept her still and pliant.

He eased even closer, shifting his body so his thighs brushed her ass. Draping himself over her spine, he sucked in air at her neck and purred. "I could make you feel better before Toby comes to lick you clean."

What?

"I know how to take a girl gentle. Is that what you want?" The pitch of his voice grew predatory, hungry. "I'll make you feel good. *Comfort* you."

Wren *couldn't* have heard him right.

Working to calm down, to gather her wits and find the strength to ignore his bone-melting purr and crawl off, she glanced through her tangled hair and found Kieran was stroking himself again… to *this*.

To her crying on the floor in a puddle of cum.

The smell of his cock, the subtle musky difference between the last offering of hard dick grew more pungent when his fist milked toward his glans. He spilled for her, just enough to change the scent markers in the air.

He even took that handful and rubbed it on her ass, delving his finger under folded legs, trying to push his juice up inside her.

A new Alpha wished to stake claim.

She should have run off, but the shock of it, of all of it, left her staring and frozen to the spot.

Deft hands went to the buttons of his shirt, Kieran pulling it wide to show a sculpted torso and the raw muscle hidden underneath. Rapacious, he teased the feel of his naked chest against her back, the purr vibrating deep into her frazzled nerves.

Wren closed her eyes.

"I can be good to you, fill you up, ease the sting." Nose nuzzling into her tangles, he licked at her ear. "Raise up that sweet ass. Good, just like that."

Why was she moving? How was this happening again?

Face to cold tile, spine arching, knees tucked under her—cum smeared and bruised.

The picture of subjugation.

Kieran didn't bother with a growl, his cock had globs of another man's sperm to offer lubrication. He didn't tease at her like Caspian had done, there was no running of his cockhead over her clit. He just slipped in.

And groaned like a wildcat ready to sup on his kill. "What did you do to him to make him act so crazy? Show me, sweet thing."

He rolled his hips in a measured stroke, stretching her around his girth until not an inch more might fit. Gyrating his pelvis against her ass, he ran his chest over her back, a full body pet both inside and out.

"What makes you purr?" The whisper

tickled her ear, the following nip to her shoulder leaving Wren shuddering. "Do you want me to stroke you, to play with your beautiful tits?"

He may have been asking, but his hands were already doing. Reaching under her, he grabbed a handful of breast, pulling at it until only her nipple was caught in his fingers. He gave it a tweak, rolling the swollen tip until she arched and her damaged throat tried to make a mewl.

A little more of his cock went inside.

"And how about this?" his fingers slipped past her belly all the way to where a little clit peeked from its hood. He strummed her there, drawing out another gasp and cramping wave of slick.

At her nervous cry, he shushed her again. "You're going to relax and let me take care of you. I know what to do." A rougher pinch sent the Omega lurching. He caught her tight, pulled her flush, and growled, "I have *every-thing* you need."

Gyrating hips stirred his cock in her channel, the steel-hard length of him rubbing at places a simple shunt in and out would miss.

Her hand slapped the floor. A plea for it to end, for him to finish tormenting her and leave her alone.

The complaint encouraged only more of the same, endless minutes of gentle enticement that left her head swimming and insides screwed up tight. It wasn't until she actively began to struggle that he broke from his pretend calm and gave her a growl more terrifying than any Caspian had used against her. It left her gushing slick around his intrusion to saturate the thatch of hair at his base and drip down her already soiled legs.

"Fuck…"

He loved it, telling her so as he growled again and again until the puddle around them grew even larger. Until Wren wasn't sure he could wring any more from her womb.

Sluicing through the river, he began to rock her back and forth. So fucking full of him, over stimulated by the dancing finger on her clit, Wren finally surrendered to his game.

He knew the instant he had won, laughing over her as he shifted from playful to gratifying. Gone were the rolling strokes, replaced by snapping hips and a pinch on her clit.

Voice husky, enunciating between thrusts, he demanded, "Are you going to purr for me?"

No…

She couldn't purr, moaning past an aching throat as she was.

"I can be as good to you as he is."

Good? Is that what these males thought they were?

Good men didn't fuck a woman on a filth-smeared floor until her knees went numb and her cheek was frozen.

And still her body responded.

She clenched around him until her ass was trembling, Kieran beginning to struggle to spear her. He had to fight convulsing muscles and a weeping slit to force his way in. And from the way the Alpha roared, he gloried in it—pulling back on her hips while thrusting forward with all his might.

He sank in deep.

Deep enough to feed her his knot whether she was ready for it or not.

It ballooned against overwrought nerves, sending her spiraling into a frenzy beyond her mental capacity to process. How had she not had enough cum? How could she feel such need for a frightening stranger just because his cock might kick inside her?

The twisting grip of her internal muscles fixed on that pulsating knot, fastening tight in a stranglehold that ran up his shaft in rippling waves.

All his talk ran dry, the male shouting gibberish as he tried to plow deeper still. Ears ringing from his roars, heart beating against her ribs, Wren whimpered as the first heavy spew was sucked from his cock to flood her cunt with seed.

Yes! *This* is what she needed to take away all reason and pain.

Another burst of fresh hot seed infiltrated her belly, held in by a still swelling knot.

An orgasm ravaged her body as more and more Alpha offering soothed the hurt, Wren unwittingly gave him what she thought to deny.

She purred.

And he grew drunk on it.

He would not let up, coaxing out rippling pressure from her clit so her orgasm might feed his. He didn't stop until she was pinned flat to the floor, the Alpha still jerking at her back fighting to push even deeper.

How long it lasted, Wren didn't know. She was still crushed under him, panting and high on the most fucked up of sex when Toby, followed by a team of Caspian's slaves, arrived.

Wren was too depleted to care she was seen lying in a pool of body fluids, naked and disgusting. But the man at her back, the one whose knot still twitched inside her, wrapped muscled limbs around her, rising up as far at the knot would allow, to snarl.

All animal, Kieran showed teeth, wild-eyed and vicious. "Get the fuck out!"

The slaves took one look at him before dropping the crates carried between them to obey.

A frowning Toby refused to budge. Not one bit intimidated, he crossed his arms over his chest and let out a low growl in response. "Down, boy. Once that knot lets up, I get to lick her clean."

Chest rumbling, Kieran narrowed his eyes. "I'm going to kill the next man who walks in here."

"Well, if that's the case, Caspian will have five workers to replace later." Toby, didn't seem to care who Kieran might kill. He cared about getting the job done. "He sent a lot a shit over for her, and I'm not going to let it sink in the mud outside."

Kieran kneaded Wren's breast, his attention going back to the knot-dazed female. "Then get it over with."

Cocking a brow, an unsettling grin growing on his face, Toby chuckled. "I'm not sure fucking her was the comfort Caspian had in mind. She looks cold and miserable."

Temper rising, his eyes snapped up. "Get me a fucking blanket then."

"There's a doctor outside with orders to see her right away. Will you be able to control yourself and not break his neck, or should I call Caspian and have him come subdue you?"

"Doctor?" As if he had forgotten the string of purple bruises blooming on her neck, Kieran carefully pulled back white hair to inspect the swelling. Unwilling to let him touch there, Wren winced, turning her face further into the cracked tile pillowing her head. "Send him in. But if I see him so much as glance at her tits the way you are, I make no promises that he'll survive it."

11

"Does it hurt when I do this?" Careful fingers manipulated the column of her throat, shifting Wren's trachea amidst blotchy, purple skin.

Sullen, trapped on Kieran's lap with his knot still thundering a heartbeat away inside her pelvis, the Omega was not in a *talking* mood.

Kieran—hardly tolerating the older Beta's presence—hissed and snarled each time the doctor touched her. "She can't speak."

Before the physician had even been permitted to approach, Kieran had lifted Wren off the icy floor, and seated them both on the couch—the knot-locked Omega propped up on his lap.

Had Toby not thought to cover her, the complete wreckage of her body would have been on display.

The old blanket stolen from her demolished nest hung over her shoulders, covering things the workers stockpiling her kitchen and the physician prodding at her neck didn't need to see. But it didn't hide the fact that Kieran's hand worked underneath, fabric tenting, the coarse cotton bobbing where his fingers chose to play.

Unable to wrest Kieran's hand away from her swollen nub no matter how hard she pulled at his wrist, he continuously teased her clit so her inner workings might cling to his knot and milk it for cum—with the old doctor right there taking her vitals and stabbing her arm for blood.

"These readings are"—the old man paused,

looking for an elegant word—"elevated. I cannot get an accurate baseline until she *calms*. And judging by her physical condition… I suggest a lighter touch. If you expect to breed her, understand that Omegas who've endured extensive physical trauma do not enter estrous."

"Breed, hmm?" The purring chest at her back expanded. Tapping a new rhythm on her clit, Kieran rasped at her ear, "You want that, sweet thing? You want me to *breed* you?"

The knot that should have been shrinking swelled even larger.

Wincing, Wren closed her eyes, only to be gathered closer so he could rock his ever-hard cock where he'd already flooded her full of sperm. With the doctor's cheeks heating and Toby licking his lips as he watched, Kieran turned her head to press a kiss to her sealed mouth. Teasing at her seam, he pushed her past humiliation and straight into another mind-killing release with only a few sure rolls of her clit and few rough bounces on his lap.

He dumped more cum inside her, hissing out an absolutely shameless groan before their audience.

The doctor cleared his throat. "I can give her a hypo-boost to speed her healing, but it will cost you—"

Toby glanced away from Wren's orgasm-drawn expression to mock the old man. "You know who had you brought here, right? Caspian wants her healthy."

The physician scoffed. "One hypo-boost is not going to make your Omega healthy. Look at her. She should be in the hospital for malnutrition. She's hardly in a better state than that boy you dropped off. The same pneumonia infects her lungs. She needs x-rays, breathing treatments, *fluids*… she's extremely dehydrated. And growing more so each time you…"

The finger tapping her clit ceased. Kieran wrapped a possessive arm around her middle, the low grate of his query threatening violence should the answer not please him. "Each time I what?"

Considering all the growls and threats on his life, the doctor remained surprisingly collected. "It requires a great deal of fluids for an Omega to endure an Alpha's attention. How long has it been since she's had water?"

Water be damned. Wren had been trying to get the doctor's attention ever since first mention of her boy. When he continued to ignore her in favor of the Alphas, she pulled her arms from the blanket to sign that she wanted pen and paper.

Kieran gave her a warning growl, immediately covering her exposed breasts with his forearm. "Behave."

She ignored him. Pleading with her hands and eyes for a tool so she could communicate.

With a nervous smile, the doctor produced a pad, clicking open the pen in his pocket before handing it over. "Tell me what hurts."

The pen moved immediately: *Do you have my Mikael? Is he better?*

Glancing at the pad she held up, the old man drew his brows together. "He's improved, yes. But it will be some weeks before he'll be off a ventilator. If he'd come to me a day later, he'd be dead. He is a very sick child who needs a great deal of care."

He would have died…

Mikael *would have died* on her couch if Caspian had not sent him to a real doctor. He still might die if Caspian's generosity ran out.

How much does his treatment cost?

The doctor said a number so astronomically high, Wren could not have paid it with ten lifetimes of constant salvage. Distressed, her insides went soft, the grumble of annoyance from the Alpha buried inside her ignored. Just as his knot was ignored so she could process the horrible realization.

She must endure Caspian and his men, survive, until Mikael was healed. Whatever it took, because she could see what the physician was not saying. If Mikael left his treatments now, he would still die. The Alpha must not grow bored of her or kill her until it was done.

Hanging her head in her hands, Wren took an unsteady breath. The pain in her body was nothing, her tattered pride unimportant. All that mattered were her boys. The price for Alec and Mikael was going to be so much more than merely whoring herself out to an evil man and his pack.

It was going to cost Wren her life.

This was debt she could never pay. When it came time to collect, she would be tossed in debtor's prison to work the quarries until her final breath.

Scrubbing silent tears from her cheeks, she went back to the pen and frantically scratched out: *Mikael is a good boy, very smart. Get to know him and you'll learn how loyal he is. Hard working. He could help you fetching things you need. Clean. Maybe you could find a safe place for him? Give him work? Please.*

Stricken, the doctor looked up from her messy words. "I can't keep the boy."

Her heart sank, but she nodded that she understood. Ten years old was awfully young to be alone and Alec was not as reliable these days as Wren might hope. Something would have to be sorted out before she was taken away. Even this home wasn't going to last much longer before it slipped under the mud.

"You're upsetting her." Kieran was pissed.

The physician could tell his time was up. "A quick injection, ice for the swelling, anti-inflammatories…" Digging in his case, the doctor produced a hypo-spray. "She'll be right in no time."

Wren tried to hand back his precious paper and pen, but the old man waved them off. "I have dozens back in the office. Keep it."

Dozens… of course he did. He wasn't forced to live in the Warrens where everything rotted.

She wrote him two final words. *Thank you.*

He didn't spare the paper a glance. With an injector placed against her jugular, he fired the mechanism. A popping sound, an unrelenting knot, and looming certain doom were the last things on Wren's mind. Swimming in the sea of happy drugs, the world was suddenly a much more comfortable place, the warm fluid flowing through her veins making everything okay.

Toby, sounding far away, snapped his fingers in her face. "What the fuck did you give her?"

"Sedation is necessary for the boost to effectively work; otherwise the pain of instant healing may lead to myocardial infarction. The effect will wear off in a matter of hours and your Omega will show dramatic improvement. She'll need rest though and"—the man glanced down at the puddle of liquid soaking into his shoe—"fluids. Give her lots of fluids."

"Hear that, sunshine?" Playful fingers tapped her knee, Toby's grin huge. "You'll be good as new before you know it."

The doctor packed up his things, and as soon as the door closed, the smirking Alpha who'd been patting her knee and keeping the blanket from slipping stood. He looked down to find that once again, Kieran was strumming her clit.

Towering over them, Toby pulled back a fist and punched the other Alpha right in the jaw. "Stop making her cum, you asshole!"

Kieran momentarily listed back from the power of the strike, sitting up with a rage-drenched roar. The knot plugging up her insides shrank in the melee, and Wren was finally set free to slip from his lap right back to the freezing puddle on the floor.

Humming in her full body contentment, certain for once that life was finally *good*, Wren lay there in a happy heap and watched two of the most massive men she'd ever seen scrap and snarl, destroying her furniture where they fought.

It was funny watching her life fall apart before her eyes, Wren's hoarse giggle drawing the raging bears to tear their claws from one another and look at her.

"She's high as a goddamn kite." Kieran curled an unhappy mouth downward. Collapsing back on the couch with his fading erection slapping against his thigh, he scrubbed a hand over his swelling eye. "You'll fucking pay for that later, Third."

"We'll see about that, motherfucker." Reaching down to gather Wren up to his chest, Toby was as cocky as a man bleeding from his mouth might be. "I did my job today, you just screwed yours."

The fight went out of the suddenly placid Alpha, Kieran narrowing his eyes. "Speaking of fucking her, *you* are not allowed to, Toby. Caspian made that clear. Take her to the nest. Clean her up. Nothing more."

Grinning down at the listless, softly

smiling woman in his arms, Toby cooed, "Ol' Toby will take good care of you."

He left his cohort, and lugged Wren down the hall, carrying her into a room that looked like hers—if hers was cluttered with alien furnishings and jugs of water. In the middle of it all was a pile of fluff that even from this distance smelled all wrong. A new nest. But it was not built from the treasures she'd found in excavation. The pillows didn't smell of her sweat and the two boys she occasionally let cuddle with her.

They didn't smell of her family.

Yet that was where the grinning Toby put her down. Reaching for a pillow, he fluffed it and said, "Should this go here, or here?"

It should go in the garbage. Had Wren the strength, she would have grabbed it right out of his hands and thrown it out the door herself. The bedding wasn't hers. It stank of male sweat and... rolling on her belly to take a deeper sniff, Wren found more than sweat marked the bedding.

Cum.

Someone had sprayed fresh seed all over the unwelcome things. The same scented seed that leaked from her pussy when she sneezed.

"Caspian and Kieran have never tended a female when they're done; they just rush them back to the pen. *I* take good care of my things. Spoil them." Toby set the pillow aside, grabbing a bottle from the piled supplies. Creeping over the naked girl, he gently rolled her to her back and gave her what might have been a charming grin if something off-putting didn't hide behind his eyes. "Thirsty?"

A drop of water on her sandpaper tongue and Wren gulped for more. Toby held the jug to her lips, allowing her to guzzle at will, sweet as could be when she came up for air. He wiped her face, praised her, continuing the process until her stomach sloshed.

Sated, she flopped back, settling into fabric softer than any she could remember—right on the cusp of drug-laced sleep.

"What a playful ray of sunshine you

are." Water forgotten, hot, searching lips found her sternum, kissing a trail lower. "That's right, smile for me. Lay back, thighs spread. Now, show me the sign for *delicious*."

The man sat back on his heels, watching the flop of her arms and repeating it. "Like this."

Wren made the sign for yes.

"How do you say no?"

She motioned with a lazy nod of her wrist, laughing so hard at his big stupid hands a wet squish of fluid leaked from her pussy.

"Look at the mess you made." He palmed the bony protrusion at her hip, tutting as a creamy dollop continue to leak from her slit. "Someone has to clean up that dirty pussy, lick you all better."

Too tired to pay him any more attention, Wren began to fade into the beauty singing under her skin—riding a high that had grown even stronger now that her thirst had been quenched—almost too euphoric to notice the slippery rasp of a spit-smeared tongue dragging over puffed flesh.

Groaning, she tried to turn away from the attention, but stronger arms prevailed.

Cracking open a lid, she found the shaved head of Toby tucked between her bruised thighs. He caught her eye, his tongue fully extended and covered in cream. Gazes locked, thoroughly wicked, he flicked up his tongue, the gob caught up into his mouth.

He made the sign for delicious.

She signed no. He signed yes.

Creeping over her where she sprawled, Toby pinched her jaw, easing it open in her daze to slowly drip the viscous mixture onto her tongue as if it were a special treat of rare candy.

Crude sounds of distress chirped from her throat until the flavor registered. Ambrosia, better than the chicken she'd devoured hours before. Caspian's cum. Kieran's cum. The spit of a man full of pheromones that spoke of virility. The three of them all laced with the sweetness of her slick.

Gobbling it down, licking at the source Wren swallowed all he offered, opening her mouth readily like a baby bird for more.

He obliged, sucking the fluids from her slit. Every drop relished with a *mhhhmmmmm* that buzzed against her and left Wren's eyes rolling back.

Lick, suck, spit. Over and over, mouthfuls of slick-laced cum gathered into his mouth so he might share it with her. On it went until his tongue scoured her clean on the inside and nothing was left for him to drip into her waiting, open mouth.

"God, that was beautiful." Lolling her head to the side, Wren found the brown haired, green-eyed man who'd *comforted* her watching from the door. Kieran sounded fully impressed as he spoke to his friend. "Even Rosie never took to your more deviant habits with a smile."

A loud, final slurp between her thighs and

Toby looked up, winking at his feast. "Still hungry?"

Snuggling down into covers that didn't quite stink as bad as they had before, Wren nodded.

Kieran stepped closer, voice firm. "Don't get carried away. Caspian's going to want her mouth first."

"You saw her nod. She's hungry." Kisses peppered her inner thighs, Toby chuckling before he took a nibble. "Aren't you, sunshine? I got plenty you can swallow."

He bit again, hard enough for pain to register past the drugs. At the sound of her yelp, Kieran flew forward and kicked the Third in the ribs.

Suction broke where teeth met thigh, and a snarling man jerked up his head to hiss. "I'm not done!"

"You're done." Challenge was there in the softness of Kieran's caution. "If Caspian sees the mark of your teeth on her skin, you'll be lucky if he doesn't break your neck. Caught in the rut, he almost claimed her today. Don't imagine he'll let you play your games with this one until he's done with her. If you want to fuck something up, fuck up Rosie."

"I don't want his castoffs any more than you do. I want *this* one! We share, that's how pack works!"

"Take up your complaint with the big guy, or be smart and wait your turn, Third. You've broken too many of your toys for him to trust you with his shiny, new whore."

Whore…

That was the last word Wren heard in her daze before she finally closed her eyes to them.

The arguments of the men continued. "But I'm hard as a goddamn rock!"

"You heard the doctor." Bored, Kieran added, "She needs her rest."

Shuffling close enough for his knees to butt her thighs, Toby growled, "She's asleep, the Omega won't even know."

"Won't know you poured a gallon of cum

down her throat? She'd fucking choke, you idiot."

The metallic clicks of a lowering zip, and Toby said, "I'll spray her tits and pussy. She should smell of my mark like she smells of you and Caspian. The boss wouldn't deny me that."

A dark chuckle came easing down into her nest. "I've never seen you so worked up over new meat."

"Coming from the man who knotted her for over an hour and would barely let me approach. You're a fucking hypocrite, Kieran."

The other Alpha had no answer.

Toby gave a final irritated grumble. "Are you going to help me, or what?"

The silence between them filled with the sound of heavy breathing and the dry brush of skin on skin.

Once or twice, guttural noises broke through Wren's haze, the Omega cracking open an eye to see the muscles in Toby's neck straining. Staring at her cunt, he kneaded his sack while the man crouched beside him stroked Toby's cock with a fury.

Four hands worked the oversized shaft, Kieran an active participant in his pack-brother's pleasure.

Half awake, she watched the skin at the base of the Third's cock began to swell, Toby pulling his fingers from his balls to grasp it and squeeze with all his strength. "Now, do it now!"

Kieran's hand flew faster over Toby's swollen cock, gripping, pulling in a way that had to hurt.

A mist of fluid splashed, Wren's face, Toby fucking into the grip of another man, gushing and gushing, until he had glazed her outsides as much as the other two had coated her insides.

He slapped his hands to her tits, rubbing in his spend while Kieran milked the last spurts of seed from the pulsating dick swinging between Toby's legs.

Her eyes drooped again as his hands smeared and kneaded.

The next time Wren woke, brown eyes—the shade of shiny mud—were inches from her own. She knew those eyes and the beast they belonged to.

Caspian brushed back the cum-crusted tangles stuck to her cheek. "Good morning, pretty mouse. Did you enjoy my gifts?"

12

She was perfection rolled up in his bedding and caked with the marks of his Second and Third. Sleepy-eyed, Caspian's mouse came awake, left languorous by the steady purr drumming from his chest.

Catching a finger under her chin, he tilted back the mouse's head to view the state of her throat. It was still smudged with marks in the shape of his hands, but no longer swollen— almost pretty, the necklace of bruises personal. His mark on her.

He kissed that flesh, the girl going rigid under his lips. "You are delicious smeared in my brothers' scents. They took good care of you, it would seem. As did I." Pulling away so he might see the effect his attention had on her lavender eyes, Caspian murmured, "Are you grateful?"

A tiny pucker formed between her brows, the Omega clearly considering the question.

She answered him with sign.

Hidden in those gestures was something less than the praise the Alpha felt he deserved. His purr cooled. "A simple nod would have sufficed."

The touch of petulance in his tone worked wonders on her expression. She gave a soft, shy smirk.

"Still under the effect of the hypo-boost, eh, mouse?"

Her pupils were set mid-dilation, the way she looked at him drowsy and sweet. It almost tempted him to let her disrespect slide.

"Since you already know what I can do to

you"—he traced his fingers over the band of bruises circling her throat—"and since I find myself contented to find my mouse in a nest provided by her Alpha, I'll give you one more chance to answer the question properly. Are you grateful for my attention and gifts?"

He didn't get the nod he'd demanded. Instead the Omega put her nose to his neck and breathed him in on a hum.

The desperate groan in response… Caspian didn't realize at first that it had come from him. Nor could he comprehend why his eyes had rolled back at the feel of her nose tracing his skin. Catching her close to him, the naked filthy thing fitting just where she should, he let her sniff and settle.

Where her little hands began a tentative exploration of chest and shoulders, his gripped all the harder. Somehow the pocket-sized thing coaxed him onto his back, and from the crook of his arm, she leaned up, somber her eyes tracing his features.

He wasn't a handsome male—never had

been—even before hard years of fighting his way to the top. But she didn't look at him as if she found him ugly, either.

She just saw a man—one she had set to purring capitulation with a few soft touches and a sniff.

Cupping his stubbled cheek in her palm, she met his eyes.

Didn't she know Omegas weren't supposed to do such things? Had she never learned her place?

Why had he not shaved before coming to her so his week-old beard wasn't between her soft skin and his scars?

The mouse mouthed the word *Mikael*, and then gave him a very discernible nod. She then took her weight from his side to sit back on her feet and sign. It didn't take a genius to grasp that the sweep of her hands meant *gratitude*.

The pretty mouse wasn't as high as he thought.

Caspian should not have relished this as much as he did, he should not have let his voice grow gritty with raw desire. "Be a good girl and show me."

Her hands settled gently on his chest, the mouse draping her torso over his bulk. Again their eyes met, hers timid and unsure.

She purred, the light trill of music only for him.

Next, her fingers went into his hair, combing through and tugging until he shuddered. They traveled lower to knead the bones of his neck, to discover the swell of his shoulders, until she could reach no further under his coat.

"Kiss me."

Her purr stuttered, but she lowered her head anyway.

Insulted, Caspian's hand flew to her hair. Taking a grip near the root, he held her lips inches away and growled, "You don't want to kiss me."

It was not a question. She didn't want to kiss him, and he was beginning to suspect she didn't want to be anywhere near him.

Grasping his other hand and dragging it to her throat, the mouse collared herself in his grip.

"You think I'm going to hurt you." Gone was his contented stupor, in its place was budding anger. "I'm tempted."

She nodded, swallowing under his palm, as if that was not the issue. Eyes wide and pleading, she blinked, waiting as if that one look might reveal her very thoughts.

It always came down to this with bitches. But he would get his, he'd get her purrs and lying smiles, even if he had to pay. Later he'd punish her until she bled for daring to bargain in the first place.

Snarling, he demanded, "Tell me what you want. I'll give it, and then you fuck me the way I want you too."

She reared back, caught around the throat and openly shaken by his words.

"Food, clean water, the blankets straight from my bed were clearly not enough!" Sitting up to tower over his caught mouse, right up in her face, Caspian roared. "Name your price, rat!"

She frantically gestured for pen and paper, pointing to a corner where a broken box stood. When he shoved her back, she raced to it, digging through her goods to unearth a cracked piece of slate and a tiny nubbin of chalk. The scrape of white on black hissed, her hands openly shaking.

She turned the board around, holding it up before her breasts for him to read, *"If you kill me, Mikael won't get the treatment he needs to survive. I was only asking you to be gentle."*

The Alpha stopped short. Narrowing his eyes, nostrils flaring on a deep inhale, he took in what her scent might offer… calculating. "You think I tried to kill you yesterday?"

She nodded, but using the heel of her hand wiped the chalk and wrote over the smear. Pointing to her tattooed cheek, she showed him her words: *I did something wrong.*

She thought it was her fault...

It hadn't occurred to Caspian the Omega failed to understand what had almost taken place. Hell, he'd expected she'd be a conceited handful now that he'd almost bonded them forever. But she didn't know, and he had no intention of giving the exotic Omega any power in knowing.

"Come here, pretty mouse."

She set the slate aside and did as he ordered.

Nervous and no longer meeting his eyes, Caspian ran the backs of his fingers over her cheek and jaw. Fragile. He could break her in half with no effort, shatter her bones with ease. Not good traits for a mate. "You want me to fuck you sweet and slow? How Kieran took you yesterday?"

Of course he'd watched it. Watched it while Rosie bobbed her slut mouth on his cock. He'd come quickly, and he'd come hard. And then he'd come again watching Toby have his fun.

The releases had taken the edge off, but the itch had not been scratched, no matter what Rosie or any of the others he'd had sent in from the pen offered.

He wanted sweet purrs and soft touches from a raw little mouse.

He wanted the blushing girl who nodded her head at his question. The girl who took his hand again and put it around her throat and rose on tiptoe to put her nose back to his throat.

Caspian was more than willing to see where this game was going. "What does my good girl do when I want to fuck?"

She purred, and by God, the Omega met his eyes.

Her stomach rumbled.

The moment was ruined by her obvious embarrassment and his unexpected laughter, but Caspian found no displeasure in it. "There is food and water. I expect you to bathe when you're done. I like seeing their cum on you, but I'm First-Alpha. They get my seconds, I don't get theirs. Afterward, you will build a proper nest to host me and I will be *gentle*."

13

<hr>

If this was gentle, Wren never wanted to know what Caspian considered rough. She'd done all he'd asked, trying her damnedest to perform. It had been easier when he'd first arrived, when the tail-end of spectacular drugs had helped keep the edge off.

Food and a great deal of water had dulled the buzz. Sponging her body off with chilly recycled water had cleared the rest of the high. He'd wanted to watch her brush the tangles from her wet hair, slipping his fingers through the dripping tresses as if fascinated with it.

When he got bored of watching her grooming, he took her by the wrist and dragged her back to her room.

He shoved her forward to the bedding. "Build the nest."

Wren had never done so with an audience. It made her nervous. Heck, the freaking hulk of man caught in a continuous growl made her nervous!

Leaning against the wall, he complained. "It's cold in here."

Considering he was dressed in that hideous coat and she'd been kept naked for days, he had some nerve. Knowing that if she acknowledged his words, if he saw her face, he'd see her spite, she kept her head bowed over her work.

"Don't you have heat? Turn it on."

Before she could stop herself, she laughed. This was the Warrens, not a penthouse mansion.

The brute picked up on her scoff and began to strip. "You have to the count of ten to finish your work. Ten. Nine. Eight..."

With an angered Alpha egging her on, Wren rushed to place the final touches. He hit *one*, and leapt upon her. She yelped from surprise, but found instead of mauling, he was pulling blankets around them to wrap them up in one another's heat.

Twisting under him, gooseflesh rubbed away by over-large hands, Wren sniffed at his neck. It was the only trick she'd found so far to calm herself when the killer was too near. The smell of him and the effect it had on her offered a much needed distraction.

She could reduce him down to the simplicity of *Alpha*. Not Caspian, the gangster with all power over Alec and Mikael's future, who shared her with his men, and almost strangled her the day before.

He seemed to like her little habit, the way she would root and pant in air. Stilling, he did the same, inhaling sharply at her ear until his chest puffed and all that warmth whooshed out over her cheek.

It set her skin to shivering, Wren offering a purr in gratitude.

Screwing up her courage, she kissed him just like he'd asked before.

A single brush of her mouth and he jammed his tongue in, chasing after hers until she figured out the rhythm. It matched the hips rocking over her, the Alpha grinding his dripping cock into the soft skin of her belly.

He'd already had her, his men had already had her, there was nothing left to lose since her pride was gone and her cause was fresh. Everything she did was for the future of her family.

She spread her legs and in synchronicity, he crawled between them.

"Did my good girl just offer her pussy?" Sucking a trail down her neck, Caspian set his teeth to her flesh. "It better be wet if she did. Bad girls tease and get fucked dry."

It was flooded, the nearness of the male as

she'd built her nest, his scent, what she knew was to come… all of it having done the job of the growl.

Easing back so he might line up his glans with her slit, the male found the scent wafting up from her was heady with Omega slick. He didn't spare her a smooth entry, his body seeming to lurch forward once alighted.

He fucked in hard.

Breath caught, Wren arched and bore it—bore him in that animal, violent spearing all the way to the hilt.

Clenching his jaw, he hissed at the clamp and flutter that had already begun. "Fuck! Don't you dare come yet, Omega!" He snapped his hips in sure, rough strokes with each word, scything into her belly so deep she lost control. "Don't. You. Dare. Fucking. Come!"

It was too late. The clench and ripple milked at this cock, leaving her moaning a pathetic breathy purr that called to him to give her what she craved. It was too far gone to stop, Wren distantly aware her body had run wildly free of her mind.

She clung to him, chasing after hips that pulled his cock away and left her cramping around nothing.

"BAD GIRL!"

Why did hearing him say that make her insides squeeze all the harder?

She sprayed out slick where his cock bobbed just out of reach, whining and writhing and denied. When the waves of needy distraction began to pass, Wren found him watching her, hovering so his cock was just out of reach.

"Didn't Kieran and Toby give you enough attention? Is your pussy really so greedy, naughty mouse?"

Dazed, unsure if she was still coming, if she needed to come, or if she wanted it all to end, Wren made a soft sound of capitulation.

"Come again before I'm ready and I'll let them both fuck your ass while my knot owns your cunt." The growl came, unnecessary at this point except to gush a fountain over his swollen cockhead. "Is that what you want, pretty mouse?"

God, was he trying to kill her with that tone? It didn't even matter what he said, her body responded… and from the smug look on Caspian's face, he knew it.

"Do you want both of them at one time while I watch?" He groaned out his fantasy, teasing at her fluttering entrance while denying the wriggling Omega what she craved. "While another woman's mouth is sucking me off?"

The heat in the nest turned ice cold.

Caspian took advantage of her alarm, slipping back in to find her pussy open and as far from orgasm as she could be.

Rocking against her, feeding her his fat dick, he murmured, "You don't need *gentle*, little mouse. You need to know your place and I need to enforce it." When she wouldn't meet his eyes, he caught her chin and pressed the subject. "Your place is to please me in any way I tell you to." Running his fingertips over the bruises on her neck, he murmured, "Mine is to make sure this doesn't happen again. You'll be grateful if another woman blows me. You'll purr when I fuck you afterward, knowing she took the edge off—because my pretty mouse excites me to the point I want to wrap my hands around her throat…"

Wren didn't think it was possible to find there was something lower than whore… but there was.

She cried as he took her *gently,* until Caspian grew frustrated with her lack of response and fucked into her with passion instead. It didn't take long for his tricks to fool her body into a mind-numbing release. She gave him what he came for, the bloom of his knot throbbing large and hot inside her cunt, thick ropes creamy white trapped behind it.

While he was contented and purring above her, she lay still, forced to accept what still spurt at random intervals from his dick.

It shouldn't have mattered. Logically she grasped that, but it did.

It hurt.

"It's easier if you understand before you come back with me." He caught her chin, something in those mud brown eyes almost repentant. "This place you live in isn't fit, and I am tired of slugging through the mud just so I can fuck you and freeze."

Then why had he brought all this stuff here? Why were they even wasting time knotted in a nest that was soon to be abandoned?

"You won't lack for attention." Voice hardly above a whisper, Caspian soothed, "Toby is already preparing your room and Kieran demands to share it. Obey them just as you will obey me." His gaze grew unforgiving, his voice sharper than razor blades. "But never forget, you are mine first and foremost. When I call, you come."

She nodded, tears drying up and heart growing hard.

Appeased, the Alpha purred, the vibration catching as another wave of filth ushered from his knot to pool in her belly. As his pleasure peaked, Caspian pressed what might have been a sweet kiss on Wren's slack mouth. "I'll be good to you."

14

"Welcome home."

This place was beyond imagining and as ugly as sin.

"Here." Toby urged her to step deeper into the room. "Come see what I chose for you."

Despite her reluctance to abandon her home, the males had made her carry an armload of the new bedding Caspian had dumped in her room. They had refused to let her bring anything personal.

They had made her march with their First Alpha's cum dripping between her legs.

They had brought her back to where it all began.

Clean water flowed through the pipeworks like drugs in a junkie's veins. It was everywhere, raining down until the air was too damp to breathe. Coughing, a deep, wracking wheeze did nothing to clear it from infected lungs.

Two minutes in, and Wren hated it here.

More importantly, she was terrified swamp-lung would fester in this environment before Mikael might be healed. She needed dry air. *Needed* it. And this place was humid with wet.

"Pretty, isn't it?"

Toby grinned as he pushed open the door, bouncing his eyebrows as if everything in Caspian's wasteland might impress her.

She made the sign for yes.

It was a lie. Her blank expression gave her away.

Expression suddenly frosty, Toby said, "You don't like it?"

Carefully placing the folded bedding on a nearby chaise, Wren took it all in. Everything looked clean, but under the smell of furniture polish was the saturated aroma of many, many males' cum and many, many females' juices. All three of her owners' scent markers were pungent.

This was their brothel where they fucked their whores. Of which she was now one.

The furnishings were rich and silly. Leather couches with deep purple pillows, a huge bed.

Wren couldn't even remember the last time she'd slept on a bed. Her nests had almost always been arranged on the ground. No way was she building one on that thing. Nope. The spot by the windows would suit her much better.

The bed could be used for other *things*, and maybe they would leave her nest alone.

Toby was still waiting for an answer, the disappointment at her lack of enthusiasm palpable. She gestured slowly, so he might see the distinct movements and possibly under-stand. "*It's big.*"

And needed to be scoured with bleach.

"Is it the color you don't like?" He crossed his arms over his chest, leaning back to the wall to glare. "I chose purple to match your eyes."

Well, that was… *sweet*? She gave him a smile, hoping it would be enough to smooth ruffled feathers.

A big purple room in which to have her body and life fucked over.

"There's clothes for you in there." He gestured to an honest-to-god armoire.

Like a good little plaything, Wren marched over, opening it up to find it was indeed stocked full… of clothes that smelled like other women. This was dress-up and she was the latest doll.

"Do you like them?"

Not even a little bit. Yet, she nodded, careful to keep her face turned away. Wren even went so far as to run her hands over random articles, pretending to admire the fabric.

She felt Toby ease up behind her, startled that she hadn't heard the Alpha cross the room. He took handfuls of her hair, holding the white strands up to his nose for a sniff.

"I like to spoil my girl. Tell me one thing you want and you'll have it." An arm slipped around her middle, his hand spreading to palm her belly. "Something pretty? A special thing that will be our secret? Hell," he chuckled, "you keep smelling like you do and I'll kill a man for you."

She let him paw and sniff, turning in his arms to motion what she needed: something to write with.

He jerked his chin toward the desk. "Write down what you want. There's paper in the desk drawer."

He let her wander over to another piece of ostentatious furniture that had no place in a random room atop the pipeworks. Coughing into her hand as she searched, Wren wrote down a simple request.

I want to see Mikael.

Scowling down at the paper, Toby pursed his lips. "I meant something special for a girl. Jewelry? Something shiny you can wear that I gave you so everyone knows that I think you're special."

Then it wasn't much of a secret was it…

There was so much more at stake here than just a shiny bauble she didn't want or need. Alec knew she'd struck a deal for his life, and when he got over his temper and returned home to find it empty… and reeking of sex, he'd sort out how to find her. But Mikael had been so sick he might not remember a thing. What if the doctor released him and he wandered home only to find it abandoned? He'd think she didn't want him.

Please.

Wry smile tugging at his lips, he tossed her pad aside. "We'll talk about the kid later. Scout's honor."

Budding anger was warring with much wiser caution, yet it still thinned her lips.

"I have something that might cheer you up." Toby cocked a grin, the sort of grin a smart girl knew not to trust. From the satchel slung over his shoulder he pulled out repurposed drapes.

Her dress.

Gesturing at the hastily donned flannel shirt and grimy pants, he purred, "I want you to take *that* off, and put this on… wear your special dress *for me*."

The memory might have been foggy, but Wren had pieced enough together to know what this man had done to her prone body while she'd healed. He wasn't waiting for a reply they both knew he'd never get. Fingers to her shirt buttons, he began to work them free.

Flannel spread, a pair of snow-white breasts unveiled. Slipping the old fabric down her arms, appreciation sparkled in overeager eyes as he licked his lips.

Palm cupping a breast, he murmured to himself. "It's almost a pity to cover these up."

After the morning she'd had, Wren was in no mood to even pretend she desired male attention. Taking the dress, she pulled it over her head and let the torn garment cover what Toby wanted to grope.

Seams had split in the days-ago tussle with Caspian, the dress no longer hanging as she'd designed it. The fabric could be mended, but, looking down at where even the skirt had rent, Wren knew it would never be the same.

Just like her.

Toby didn't seem to mind. He took her fingers and spread her arms wide, looking over the figure she cut. "You'll wear this when it's just us, huh? For me only. The others won't understand."

Wren nodded.

Grin going wider, he leered. "And the room? You really don't like it, do you? Tell me what you want and I'll have it changed."

Was he being playful, or was this some kind of duplicity? He'd taken her pen and paper, leaving communication closed.

Winging her answer, Wren took a step back, gestured between them, and began to slowly sign the alphabet. If he really wanted to give her something, he could give her a way to communicate.

After all, of her three owners, he was the only one who'd asked what signs meant and actually watched her hands when she spoke. Making a game of it, just as when she'd taught the boys, Wren teased with little pokes and sly smirks, shaping his fingers into the sign for 'A'.

Toby was a fast learner, one who stole a kiss every time he got a gesture right. By the time they reached 'Z', the lesson took on a different aim. Armoire at her back, panting Alpha pressed to her front, the shaft trapped between them began to thicken and grow.

"He's going to let me fuck you tonight," the male breathed over her neck, licking at the remaining bruises like a cat cleaning his young. "You're gonna like it. He thinks you won't, but I know you will. My playful ray of sunshine can handle Toby's knot in your sweet little pussy. She can take all I give her."

A growl rumbling from his ribs, Toby hiked up her skirt to slip his fingers into her panties. The fabric stuck to where warmth flowed at his call, peeled away so he might prod the source.

"Caspian likes them obedient. Kieran likes them fawning. Me? I like you. Just like this. Honest, wet, and ready for me." Fingers squelching through the trickle, he fed her pussy as much as he might. Rubbing at her insides, pushing almost to the point of pain, he said, "I won't touch the other girls like they will. You'll get all my attention."

If that was a threat or a promise, Wren couldn't tell. She could hardly focus on any-thing but what he was doing between her legs. It wasn't all sexual and it felt a little strange… as if he was *stretching her*.

Pressing his forehead to hers, he closed his eyes, scissoring his fingers inside her body. "God, you're tight. I'll have them both take you first… make you ready."

What on earth was he talking about?

Breath catching, Wren went to her toes when Toby angled his hand and pressed upward. Her discomfort was noted, but not alleviated.

He growled, using her bodyweight to prod deeper, undulating his hand. Slick came at the rumble in the Alpha's chest, but arousal was stalled… like his hand in her pussy that could go no further.

"I'll stop when you let me put my fist in. I'll stop when I feel you squeeze it like a knot." The way he breathed, how his chest rose and fell with excitement, it was as if *he* were bordering on climax. Not her.

Just from *touching* her. Touching her in a way that was more pain than pleasure. It didn't feel like a cock or a knot, not when he circled his wrist and stretched what wasn't ready.

Labia tingled and burned.

She hissed and he groaned, Toby humping against her hip until the scent of cum tinged the air. In the midst of his awkward climax, he speared his hand all the way to the knuckle of his thumb, and murmured, "You little tease. Keep making those pretty noises for me."

Trying to climb him to relieve the pressure, Wren hung about his neck and hitched a leg to his hip. He groaned all the harder, grinding the bulbous growth at the base of his shaft against her leg.

Without pressure engulfing his knot, Toby's release was short-lived. It ended after a few scented spurts. The Alpha smiled at the woman hooked on his fingers with pure wickedness. "Do you know what happens to an Alpha who denies his knot?"

Wren shook her head, eager for his fingers to retreat.

"A buildup of fluids accumulates; the knot deforms and fails to shrink. It won't go away completely until I drain it… which I won't be doing. Instead I'm going to half-cum over and over all day until my cock is swollen and my balls are ready to pop. Tonight, after Caspian and Kieran have stretched your sweet pussy and filled you with cream, I'm going to shove the special knot I'm preparing just for you right past these tight lips. I'll fuck you for however many hours it takes for your perfect pussy to squeeze me all the way down. And you're going to take it, all of it, until no other knot will ever make you feel like mine did."

Knots had to expand inside an Omega; it couldn't be pushed in already formed…

He was going to hurt her like the Alpha who took her virginity had when he'd torn his knot out.

"Shhhh…" He began to wiggle his fingers again, returning to stretching her opening. "It will only smart a little… and then it will feel very good. You'll see. I'll be your favorite in no time."

Closing her eyes to the burn when he again tried to push deeper, Wren tried to relax so this might end.

"Bear down. Good, just like that. I'm not leaving until you take my whole fist."

15

———————

Toby had been unable to work his whole fist in, at least not while Wren was still on her feet. Now that the bed was at her back, purple bunting hanging from the ceiling like she was a god-damn princess, the Alpha had made a little more progress.

"So patient." He kissed her belly, rubbing his shaved head against the soft skin. "Just a little more."

He'd stripped her naked, folding the dress with care before he set it aside. After he'd laid her down, he'd left her spread so wide Wren should have felt shame. She might feel it later, once the anxiety and discomfort passed.

The bed began to rock again, Toby stroking himself to another unfulfilling orgasm. The knot he'd warned her about was angry and pulsing in so many places that it looked alive—writhing under his flesh in a twisting convulsion of blood vessels. Hand moving faster on the unmangled part of his dick, a light spray of warm seed hit where his fist was *almost* buried inside her, the Alpha hissing, straining from the pain.

Why would he do this to himself?

More importantly, how did he think that *thing* was going to fit in her body?

There was something very wrong with a man who would subject himself to hours of self-torture chasing after a disfigured cock. *The knot* wasn't a knot at all anymore. Halfway up his already huge dick, it rippled and ridged. Like rolling blobs of veined corruption.

As it grew a little larger, Wren grew more afraid.

The scent of fear in her sweat drew Toby's attention away from his self-imposed agony. Blue eyes gentled, the lines that had pinched at the corners during his climax softening. "You'll learn to love the pain… to anticipate what only I can offer." He began to stroke himself again. "Be willing, soft and open, long enough for me to get inside, and I'll take you to heights you can only imagine."

It wasn't possible.

When Caspian had fucked her, it had taken the Alpha several minutes just to ease his cock fully into her body. That thick, long, and daunting member… Wren had required purrs, enticing growls, and patience before he could even thrust in balls deep.

The pulsating mass between Toby's legs would never, *ever* fit.

Huge fist stretching her cunt opening, or no.

When she fruitlessly tried to wriggle back, the fingers already inside her balled up, changing the shape of his unholy invasion. Body trembling, her cunt flexed automatically in a bid to pull the false knot deeper. It knew the placement was wrong. That the feeling of fullness was a lie.

God, it burned!

Head thrashing back and forth, Wren began to cramp. "Uuuungh."

"Good girl. Just a little bit more."

No attention had been paid to her clit, yet it was stiff at attention, begging for anything that would ease the stretch. Desperate for relief, Wren plucked at the swollen nub, uncaring if Toby saw.

The man jerked his fist on his cock all the harder, another mist of cum landing where she worked. "Fuck that's hot."

Fire burned between her legs, heat twisting her spine and abused hole until the licking flames stole her breath. Orgasm latched onto Toby's fist, and sucked him in a ripple of overabundant sensation all the way to his wrist.

Finally…

A fist was not a knot, but the bumps of his finger bones felt so fucking amazing as she came undone that the searing stretch at her cunt mouth hardly registered. He pumped his fist, making her insides chase after what they tried and failed to milk until she was delirious.

Thrashing on the bed, she rode a man's fucking hand until not a single ounce of pleasure was left to wring out.

The slick that slopped out when he carefully unfurled his fingers and left her poor pussy alone became his feast. It saturated the bed, soaking down to the mattress to mingle with the layered scents of other women's sex, making her degradation a part of this place.

Monster dick too swollen and gnarled to jut upwards, Toby crawled over her, the *thing*, dragging over her body like a third leg. He kissed her bitten lips, purring loud to soothe the troubled, aching girl.

It took him time to calm her, loud purrs and soft strokes. Words of praise. Sweet flattery. Minutes of cuddles and kissing away tears. When she grew quiet and focused enough to pay attention, Toby put his lips to her ear and announced, "Next time, two fists."

She wasn't supposed to say no, but Wren was already vehemently shaking her head.

It seemed she had an ally. From the door, Kieran barked, "No fucking way is Caspian going to let you do that to her. He ordered you to prepare her if you were going to use that thing on her, not rip her apart. She could hardly handle one fist. Two would leave lasting damage."

Sitting back, Toby grinned his triumph. "She came without anything but a few growls and my hand."

"Bullshit. She touched her clit."

"Her orgasm had already begun. I followed Caspian's rules, and she creamed all over my fist." Hefting his mangled cock to display its monstrous girth to his friend, Toby smirked. "When you see her take this thing later, you'll wonder why you've never tried it."

Kieran grimaced. "My dick hurts just looking at that freakish thing."

As the two bickered, Wren turned away and climbed off the bed.

It had been a long day, and from the sound of it, it would be an even longer night. Uncaring if they called to her, she took up the nesting materials brought over from her house and began to craft a place of safety.

With the covers still pulled over her head, wrapped in comfort only a nest could offer, Kieran kneeled at her side. "The bed is for you to enjoy, Omega. You don't have to sleep on the floor."

She *wanted* to sleep on the floor.

Hard surfaces were familiar and the distinct smell of other women's pussies was far enough away that she could almost forget the taint wafting in the air. Moving the covers so that Kieran might see her face, she pointed at her nose, pointed at the bed, then pointed at her nose again while squishing her face up in disgust.

"It smells bad?"

She nodded emphatically.

The Second stood tall, walking over to the purple monstrosity to sniff the air. Confused, he leaned down and pressed his nose right to the covers. "Smells good to me."

Of course it smelled good to him, he was breathing in years of sexual conquests... probably reliving some fond memories. Alphas were sluts. Omegas were territorial. If she had to stay in the pipeworks to keep their bargain, she didn't want to sleep on that.

She wouldn't be *able* to sleep on that.

When he stomped over, green eyes snapping, Wren cut him to the quick. She reached for him, invited him in a hastily organized nest that smelled of only one female. Begrudgingly he took the bait, stripping off his shoes to settle for a moment's rest beside her.

Toby sat on the bed watching, still working his disgusting dick. He was ignored, dismissed when she gave him her back and wrapped Kieran's arm around her middle.

Nose in her hair, protesting the discomfort of an unyielding floor, he pressed against her back. "Only this once."

This life had to be lived one moment at a time. It was the only way to keep sane in the Warrens, and the only thing that would get her through these coming weeks in the pipeworks. So Wren took this moment and stole comfort from the Alpha still grumbling at her back.

Sinking into his warmth, purring for him so he might be tempted to purr for her, she closed her eyes and refused to dream.

Dreams only made reality hurt that much more.

16

Arm asleep and shoulder throbbing, Kieran cracked open an eye. The Omega snored out a lazy purr, her lips parted and appealing. Very appealing.

She shouldn't be… considering.

Yes, she was pretty, but so were most of the women in the pen. Hell, Rosie was fucking beautiful—full hips, red lips, and tits that he could bounce a quarter off of. Caspian's mouse was… scrawny, inexperienced.

But she *smelled* amazing.

Her little hesitations were fun, the look in

her eye as she discovered what Alpha cock really offered…

Goddamn perfection.

All her white hair, once it had been cleaned with actual soap and untangled, would turn heads for miles around. Just like those albino lavender eyes. Kieran would wager no other woman over half the planet had eyes like that.

And he did like to gamble.

Bets had already been placed, in fact. His money was riding on Rosie scratching her way back to Caspian's lap and First-Alpha selling this one to a high-profile connection. His mouse was too unique to set free, and no matter what Caspian might have promised her, he wasn't going to let a rare commodity slip back into the mud. Caspian's mouse would be mated and fat with a baby in six months, tops.

Smirking, growing warm by the idea of her growing round, Kieran pondered if it should be *his* baby slipped in that belly before she was passed off. Her new owner didn't need to know she was already seeded. Get him drunk enough the night of the claiming and none would be the wiser.

After seeing her invade the pipeworks just to fetch two boys… after watching her face down the meanest fucking Alpha on the planet, Kieran knew she'd never dare tell. This Omega would protect her brood at any cost.

Imagining a kid growing up in one of those fancy houses, lording over a city of morons… never knowing his good looks came from a reviled gangster daddy. What a laugh.

Of course, all of these potentialities would go to shit if Toby got clingy. The Third was like a dog with a bone—a weird, overswollen, boner, more like. The Third had almost started a war over a Beta Caspian refused to let him keep. The problem had sorted itself out when Toby took things too far and she ended up dead as a doornail.

Kieran had seen the corpse.

That fucking deformed knot… Toby had taken it too far.

Leave an Alpha unappeased and riled with backed up cum, and turns out his mind might snap. Instinct took over until urges found release.

Which is why Caspian and Kieran would be right there tonight. Fuck, Kieran would have been there regardless. It was sure to be a hell of a show, but he still wasn't sure why Caspian was allowing it… on the girl's first day.

Unless he wanted her broken in, finished, and set aside quickly.

Even a whore as willing as Rosie only had to do *that* once—and only after she'd been shared between them for months. The way she'd whined afterward had been the end of it. One thing Caspian refused to tolerate was a woman's whiny mouth.

Punished for all that bitching, Kieran was pretty sure Rosie hadn't been allowed to draw breath until every last member of the gang had been sucked dry… even the Betas Rosie thought were beneath her.

Omega females were so damn presumptuous. Even this one, who'd conned him into sleeping on the floor.

He gave her shoulder a shake. "Omega, it's time to wake up."

The snoring caught on a snort, totally unladylike and almost endearing. It shouldn't have made him smirk, but it did, and that annoyed Kieran enough that he pushed her onto her back and scowled. "You will not sleep on the floor in this room. You will sleep on the bed with me. I don't care if you hate the smell."

The woman yawned, sleepy-eyed as she reached up to pat his cheek.

It was the first time she'd touched him in any way slightly intimate that he had not initiated… and that too irritated him. Rosie was on him every chance she could get. Fuck, all the bitches in the pen were.

And this one thought to make him sleep on the floor?

"Next time you try to lure me with female tricks, remember this. Caspian didn't want you in his room. I claimed you so Toby couldn't fuck with you all night. Show some goddamn gratitude or I'll dump you in the pen to sleep alone like the other whores."

That word. That one hissed word, and the Omega went ragdoll still.

Snide, showing his face to best advantage, Kieran sneered. "You think of yourself as something other than a whore?"

She swallowed, blinked, and refused to shake her head.

"You just let a sexual deviant jam his fist into your pussy with no complaint. I watched. I liked watching. Just as much as I'll like watching your cunt eat up the treat he has in store later."

Nothing.

Wait. Was she… was she actually crying?

Arms bulging, smooth chest puffed, he

didn't allow her to move when she began to try to wriggle free. Instead he kept her pinned like a worm on a hook and watched her fail utterly at escaping his weight.

The alteration in her scent didn't please him nor did the sensation pinging at his ribs when she made her sad, little sounds. "What did you imagine was going to happen when you made your trade?"

Kieran really wanted to know, completely befuddled by this behavior—Omegas were designed to serve Alphas. They *wanted* to. Rosie had been begging for his cock only this morning.

Living with him was better than starving in a freezing shit-box and trading scrap for half a credit and some rotting food.

Sitting up just enough so she might weasel away, Kieran saw the look in her eyes. Hurt. It wasn't pouting because he'd commanded she do something she didn't want to. It was honest to god pain.

"Answer me."

The part of her that he caught when she'd been half awake and content, this is what she'd hidden under the *silence*. Raw… just like Caspian had said.

"It was bound to happen one way or another, you must know that. Stamped face or no, some male was going to find a use for you. Make the best of who claimed you first. For a few months you'll live like a queen. You'll have food. You'll have water, and baths, and attention. Nod that you understand."

She did, but the look in her eyes was not gratitude or even excitement at the prospect. The Omega was *resigned*.

"Do you know how many whores in the pen would spill blood to be in your shoes right now?"

The shake of her head and the accompanying expression was not provoking, yet still his irritation grew. It was clear she sensed it. Those violet eyes glanced down in submission, her posture changing from defensive to meek.

"If you think I'm going to fall for that, you're playing with the wrong Alpha." Climbing to his feet, he pulled her up after him. "You're here for one reason. Tonight you'll feel a reminder of it… and tomorrow, you'll build your fucking nest on the bed."

Water up to her chin, enough to drink for a week, sloshed warm and lovely every time she moved a muscle. This is what heaven had to be. All the flesh that stung was soothed, tense muscles were rendered jelly. Wren didn't even care that what had started crystal clear was dingy gray once she'd settled in. For the first time in five years, every speck of mud was going to be off of her.

And there was soap. Soap!

Things to clean her hair. Another bottle to soften it.

These precious items would have cost her three month's income. They would have been stolen from her house had anyone in the Warrens known she possessed them.

She ran the bar over her shoulder for the third time, purring like a well-fed cat.

Who knew something as simple as a bath could heal so much?

The morning had been difficult. If she let herself ruminate over how completely fucked she was, she'd start screaming. The evening was going to be worse. She was going to be shared by all three of them. Something larger than a fist was going to tear through her body for the pleasure of a gangster she only knew by reputation and insinuation. All her fear had to be crammed into a little box in her head. The lid shut tight.

Warrens rats lived only in the moment, and took the small pleasures a hard life offered. She took the bath and relished every finger pruning moment.

Right now, she was a sleek mouse. One who'd been fed more food than she could hold. Who had swallowed not two, but *three* glasses of clean water. One who was still alive.

Whose boys were still alive.

The moment had to be savored. Small victories had to be enjoyed.

Even when the steam exacerbated her cough, she didn't mind. Purring as loud as her tight chest might allow, she dunked her head and doused all that hair with shampoo. Bubbles, glorious bubbles, ran down her temples.

It was scentless, made for Omegas—so her natural odor would not be spoiled by perfume.

And it felt wonderful.

The Alpha who'd brought her here watched from the door. The creeper…

Always spying, that one. In the handful of days she'd known him, Kieran had watched

Caspian fuck her. Watched Toby lick her. Watched Toby fist her.

And now he watched her take a bath.

Of all the moments he'd witnessed, this one seemed to intrigue him most. Not that Wren was paying him any mind. There wasn't much to like about the good-looking one. And he didn't seem to like much about her. Yet still he'd hovered all day, buzzing his irritated purr at her side like a mosquito looking to bite.

Gathering her hair at her nape, Wren drew the suds down, pulling the tangled locks over her shoulder so she might scrub what hung down to her waist.

It was too long. A constant reminder of another sad day in her life.

Maybe it was time to cut it... considering the reason she'd let it grow long.

A remembrance of someone special lost to her. The one who had pulled her out of the mud.

But not now. Not here with *these* men.

When it was over and she was home with Alec and Mikael, all of it would go.

Inching forward so she might lean back and dunk her hair, for a brief moment lavender eyes met green. Brief, because she immediately lowered her lashes and submerged. Underwater was a different place, with different rules and no males in it to spoil the whoosh in her ears.

Soap dissolving, years of dirt floating away on that wave of warmth, Wren indulged until a coming cough urged her to break the surface.

As air tore from ailing lungs, Wren ignored the sharp pains and foul taste of what came up. Those things were not allowed in this moment. Those things had to wait.

"Catch your breath." The Alpha invaded her peace, coming over with a small square of clean towel. He held it up for her to spit into. He even looked at what came up. "No blood, that's good."

No. No blood. Not yet at least.

Considering his behavior from before, Wren jerked when the male began to push wet hanks of clean hair off her face. "Do well tonight and I'll take you to the doctor in the morning. We'll let him take a look at you, and… you can see your boy."

She grabbed his wrist with a strength that made the Alpha's eyes go wide. Tugging it to make sure he was paying attention, she nodded enthusiastically.

"I ain't saying he'll fix you. You don't sound so good."

Who cared if he fixed her? Shaking her head, squeezing his wrist all the tighter she mouthed the word, *Mikael*.

It seemed to dawn on him what this really was about. "You want to visit the child…"

Yes! More than anything.

He seemed to grasp the leverage the situation offered. "You'll nest properly on the bed?"

Yes!

"You'll greet me with a smile and kiss, the way a fancy Omega pleases her mate?"

Forever, if that's what it took.

"I'll make a bet with you. You play along with what we want to do to you tonight. Fuck Caspian like you did on the couch—I better see his eyes roll back." Fingers splaying on the back of her skull, Kieran give her a winning smile. "Make no complaints when Toby takes his turn. You take *everything* he gives you with all the enthusiasm you can muster. Do that, sell it, and I'll take you to see your kid."

The men's evening entertainment was going to happen either way, but the whole horrible scenario was made more palatable if there was some tangible reward. Wren pressed her wet forehead to where his hands rested on the lip of the tub and nodded.

He hadn't mentioned what he wanted sexually for himself, and that made a slow creep of warning itch up her spine. Men like Kieran, didn't just want to be smiled at and kissed. He was going to make a demand. And it was going to be something she would hate.

She would do it with a goddamn smile if it meant even five minutes with Mikael.

CLEAN, so clean that even her fingernails didn't hide a trace of dirt, Wren played dress up. Her hair had been brushed free of snarls, left to hang like a waterfall of white down her back. Kieran had painted her mouth with shine, the slip on her lips strange and tasting of cherries.

It had been years since she'd had cherries.

"Stop rubbing them together, you'll ruin the effect."

She obeyed, stealing one last lick when the Alpha turned his back to grab another other oddity from the armoire.

The devilish glitter in his eyes when he turned let her know she'd been caught. "You'll be punished for that later."

Pressing her hands together in supplication, Wren took a step toward him, ready to beg.

"Our deal still stands." The male smirked and stood his ground when she put her hands to his chest, pleading with her eyes. "I'll take you to the doctor, if you win our bet."

Before she might back away, he swooped down and tasted her lips, sucking them clean until every last molecule of cherry flavor had been stolen. Arms fixed around her middle, the purr he pressed into her was of a different nature than the ones he'd lavished upon Wren before. Nothing like the rattle after Caspian had wrung her neck or the hum when the Second had fucked her. Different than the irritated buzz that had filled the air in the nest and followed her about all day.

This was rich and masculine… expectant. This was from a different person entirely.

This was appealing.

Play the game… be his *fancy Omega*.

She was already dressed in soft blue, already scrubbed clean and new. How hard could it be to play for one night?

Wren let Alpha music work upon her, opening her mouth to him. Even groaning when his tongue stole in.

A fancy Omega like the ones thriving in the upper levels, with mates who loved them and children who didn't starve before their eyes. It was a dream she could easily fall into, just as she melted into Kieran's arms.

Wren had spent a lot of time pretending since she'd been cast down into the mud. She was good at it. Pretend life wasn't so awful.

Compartmentalize. Survive.

The purr she made was honest in the sense that it rang out with true hunger even if it wasn't for this male. She *was* hungry. For life. For safety the strong arms wrapped around her could offer. For a future.

She kissed him back, eager and willing to play house if only for a few moments. She kissed him back and lied to herself.

Husky and warm, Kieran broke away,

blinking down at the thing in his arms. "That was… that was good."

A soft smile back was offered. It had been good. Considering the man and how much she disliked him, it had even *almost* felt real.

In a heartbeat, his expression cleared of bewilderment, skepticism inching into those piercing eyes.

Skepticism was a second language to her.

Signing, knowing he couldn't understand and would make no effort to, Wren let her fingers dance. *"I want to be happy too. I never wanted to be abandoned, to bury children, to live one hungry day to the next. You want a fancy Omega? That's a game I can play."*

"What did you say?" he cocked his chin toward the pad of paper on the desk. "Write it down."

Lips wistful, she shook her head, signing, *"It means this."*

Wren stepped forward again, put her lips to his mouth, and gave him a very real kiss. One she wished she could give to another.

18

Wren hadn't paid much attention to her surroundings when she'd been brought into the Pipeworks, lugging an armful of goods. She'd kept her head down, embarrassed… knowing everyone who saw her pegged the exact reason Caspian marched her forward.

That they could smell it was his sperm that had leaked out and soaked her pants.

But it was different now that she had been prepared for him *and* his pack. They stared, and she had no blankets or shapeless clothes to hide behind. All she had was Kieran, who she clung to as if he weren't the cause of her humiliating parade.

He didn't seem to mind her arms entwined around one of his, or how she half-hid herself against his body. "None of them will touch you."

Bullshit. Men didn't look at a woman like that unless they were damn well planning to touch them.

Christ, if these men with Caspian's symbol, the black hand, engulfing the lower half of their faces found out where she lived when this was over, she would be literally and figuratively screwed.

And this couldn't be over soon enough.

The room Toby had prepared for her wasn't exactly close to Caspian's. The walk involved changing levels, various halls and corridors, a complete change in scenery back to the gritty underbelly of the water filtration plant Caspian controlled.

He lived in the thick of it, away from the lush corridors upstairs.

Guards flanked an ominous door across a catwalk, so high above the churning systems below, that Wren kept her eyes locked straight ahead. One stupid glance down and all that water Kieran had made her drink would come back up.

Her courier noticed the hesitancy in her steps. "You'll get used to it. Close your eyes if you want. I won't let you fall."

What was worse? Keeping them open and knowing what was ahead, or trusting the smirking gangster at her side?

"I can carry you across… just this once."

No way. Shaking her head, stinking of dread, Wren took that first step. Because that's how life was. No one was going to carry you, unless there was a price. And Wren had already bought more than she could afford.

The door was almost within reach when Kieran pulled her to stop. "Wait."

Perking her ears, Wren heard what had stopped their progress—very vocal sounds of a man at the cusp of orgasm.

Caspian.

The muffled grunts came to an end, the male words that followed dampened by concrete walls and that guarded door, indecipherable.

The portal ahead slid open. A woman wiping a lipstick-smeared mouth still dripping with cum stepped out.

She was a beauty if ever there was one. Buxom, tall. Dressed to appeal, and even sporting expensive cosmetics on her face. Caspian's scent wafted from her, as did the sweet smell of Omega slick.

This specimen was what all men wanted.

The stunning blonde startled when she found an audience waited, and what had been a victorious smile turned into a glower. "Who are you?"

It was always awkward when someone

asked her name, Wren already pointing to her mouth and shaking her head.

Kieran answered for her. "This is Jax."

Hand to her hip, licking up a dribble of cum at the corner of her mouth, the beauty smiled again. It was not friendly. "It's always good to meet a new girl. I look forward to some chit chat when you get to the pen. I'll show you the ropes."

"She can't speak, Rosie." Kieran was enjoying this exchange, his saucy response making no secret of it. "And this one isn't sleeping in the pen. Caspian put her up in the big room."

The woman scoffed. "Yeah, well, he put me up in the big room at first too." Lashes darkened by smeared mascara, fanned down, Rosie taking a good, long look at the tattoo on Wren's cheek. "We'll see how long you last."

Kieran tutted, a playful bend to his voice. "He's given you more than he ever gave the others. Don't be sore."

"I get it. She's punishment for mouthing

off last week. Message heard loud and clear, Captain." She saluted the male, even winked provocatively before turning back to Wren and shrugging. "I've already sucked him off twice. I doubt he'll even touch the *defective* merchandise."

One could only hope.

The blonde edged nearer, pinching Wren's blue hem. "That's my dress…"

Kieran spoke the woman's name softly but with clear warning. "Rosie."

Blue eyes made extra bright by open invitation darted up to dance over Kieran's smile. "I haven't seen you all day. Walk me back, would ya, handsome? I'll make it worth your trouble."

A male hand landed with enough force against Wren's ass to smart. "Head on in, sweet cheeks. Tell Caspian I'll be back later."

And like that, Wren was abandoned before the lion's den.

Blinking at the guards, not sure what to make of the feminine giggles and male laughter at her back, she let go a long, troubled sigh.

In the blink of an eye, clean skin and a borrowed blue dress were no longer special. Stomach in knots, she could no longer pretend. Not after those few awkward minutes with Caspian's woman.

They already had an Omega, *a perfect Omega*. Wren had no idea where that left her or why she was here.

The nervous habit of touching the tattoo left her fingers pressed to her cheek, teeth worrying her lower lip.

The taste of cherries was no longer a treat.

Behind that door was a man who'd just had another woman, who had been sated *twice*. A man she'd sold herself to, who'd taken her from her home only this morning so he *wouldn't have to slog through mud to fuck her*.

A man who had Mikael taken to a doctor and saved his life. How did one come to terms with such a dichotomy?

Both guards openly watched her standing there, one kind enough to say, "You don't have to knock. He's expecting you. Go in."

She knocked anyway, buying a few precious seconds before she was faced with whatever confusing reality was beyond that door. After an agitated grumble, the door was yanked back, an irritated, shirtless Alpha leaning against the frame.

He took a long look at her standing there alone, dressed in blue, clean, with fresh shiny gloss on her lips. "Mouse."

She nodded once at his greeting, signing hello.

"Where's Kieran?"

Wren looked over her shoulder and back, peals of feminine laughter ringing out from the nearest corridor.

"Hmmmm."

She wasn't sure why, but the petulant look in his eye made her smirk. Offering the same purr she would have given a moody Alec, Wren stepped forward, ready to be off of the lofty gangway and perched in a room reeking of a man who did not require her attention.

Small blessings and all that.

He let her pass under his arm, giving her hair a not so subtle sniff.

The inside was not what Wren had expected. Masculine, yes, but tidy. Well, organized chaos more like. Papers stacked up, piles of books, clutter. A large bed dominated one wall, a leather armchair facing it. A nearby table, large enough to seat eight, sported a half-eaten plate of food and a bowl of something unidentifiable.

"That's for you, pretty mouse."

By the size of dainty teeth marks in the sandwich, Wren knew whose leftovers these were. They belonged to the same woman who had left her discarded, pheromone laced underwear on the floor. But food was food, so she reached forward.

"Not that." Caspian jerked his chin toward the bowl of wiggly mush. "That."

Wren would have rather eaten the sandwich, but took a chair and lifted the waiting spoon to taste green slop. It didn't have a flavor worth mentioning… though it had a lot not worth mentioning. Slimy, it squished on her tongue, going down like swallowing a live slug.

Eyes darting back to the plate with a sandwich and beautiful, fat grapes, Wren swallowed another bite.

There must have been an unpleasant expression on her face, for Caspian narrowed his eyes, and growled, "It's supposed to be good for you. And you'll eat it all, every day."

Spoon in her mouth, she offered a conciliatory smile. Food was food, and she was grateful. Displaying her gratitude the only way she know he might grasp, she ate with vigor. Which was honestly easier—swallowing quickly dulled a portion of the non-taste.

"Good girl." When the last glob was swallowed, Caspian pointed to a pitcher under a dripping spout. "Water is there. You can drink as much as you want."

Kieran had said something similar when he'd fed her lunch, but it was still an almost jarring thing to hear. *All the water you want, whenever you want.*

The Alpha obviously expected her to drink some now, so Wren stood and filled two glasses. Handing one to him, she saw bewilderment on his face. But he took the cup and drained it as she drained hers.

"Have you had enough?"

She nodded.

"Good. I'm tired of waiting." Snatching her empty cup from Wren's hands, Caspian tossed them to patter over the table, and was on her a second later. Back to the wall, hot Alpha muscle melting her front, she gasped in surprise and found his tongue twisting into her mouth.

She'd heard him climax. Smelled both his cum and a foreign Omega's arousal in the air.

She'd seen the slick-soaked, discarded panties left by the leather chair!

What was he doing?

Yanking too hard at the zipper on the pretty blue dress led to the sound of tearing seams and another gasp. Fabric fell off one shoulder, hot lips fastening to uncovered skin long enough for her to draw breath.

An endless Alpha growl worked against her shock, the pooling slick in the gusset of her panties already overflowing to trickle down pale thighs.

That's what he was after…

Her scent.

Caspian ran his hands through it, spread it over her hips, her ass. He rubbed it into blue fabric. In two minutes flat, he made a soggy mess of her.

Clit throbbing, head swimming from the way he continued to take her mouth, Wren began to whine for mercy from that unrelenting growl. Her pussy was already pooling with slick, her body responding exactly as it should have. But still he continued to rumble out a call.

Female fingers went over his mouth in a bid to silence him. He bit her, growling all the louder.

Enough had been done to her today that this endless rumble, something so simple as a noise, was enough to set her insides to choke on nothing. It wasn't an orgasm; it was a bid for mercy amidst her total confusion.

Yes, his hand gripped her ass. Yes, a warm palm kneaded a blue-draped breast. But where he was focusing his attack was painfully ignored.

Punishment?

Was this for knocking at his door and making him get up to answer? Or for pulling a face at his generous offer of food?

Hooking her leg at his hip she ground against his knee and could have groaned in agony when it was not enough.

Not so long as he made that noise.

His hand when to his fly. The male who

smelled of another woman, whose cock was most likely still smeared with her red lipstick, was going to fuck her like this, in the most degrading way imaginable.

Wren grew angry. Barking a growl of her own, she shoved him back.

Panting, eyes wild and pupils enlarged, the Alpha roared, "Are you telling me no?"

She put a hand to his thumping heart and tried to catch her breath. Suffocating on the heady stink of ardent Alpha, the lingering reek of another Omega, her own slippery offering, her body's response was a jangled mix of instinctual demands.

Present, be fucked. Reject, protect yourself.

"I gave you food and water!"

Wren closed her eyes, unsure why the room was spinning.

"Shelter. My finest room!"

She nodded, straining her neck forward so she might take a breath of him and be calmed.

Though he practically vibrated with agitation, he let her nose his chest, barking, "Why do you do that? The others don't. They strip like good whores and bend over."

The reminder was a necessary one. It didn't matter if she was overwhelmed, if she was half-sick with the stink in the room, if she wanted it or not. She wasn't here to enjoy what he did, just to bear it.

Fingers went to the straps of her dress, pulling them down her arms until the garment might slip on its own and pool at her feet. Wren didn't meet his eye when she shucked the sodden panties next. She just stood there, waiting for a command.

Like a real whore.

When he made no move to direct her, when he failed to touch, she peeked up under her lashes and found him glowering something fierce.

"Next time you push me away, I'll take what I want in a way you will not enjoy. Do you understand me, trembling mouse?"

She displayed her understanding by

reaching for his belt. Perfunctory, pulling it open as if she'd done so a thousand times, Wren parted his fly. There it was, red smears of what had probably been very pretty lipstick.

The shudder that followed, she couldn't have checked no matter how hard she might try.

Still, her hands went to lift that beast, the throbbing of a still engorging cock almost hypnotic. Under her palms, it beat in rhythm to his heart, set the pace for her breaths, and grew all the larger.

She'd never touched a cock before. There had never been a need to. Touching one now, smearing her fingers in the red until the pads had been stained, she held them up. Another woman's mark on a man who used many. A man who had begun to grumble out a purr mutilated by more of that demanding growl for her slick.

Looking from her stained fingers to his eyes, she took that hand and smeared red right over his heart… so she wouldn't forget when her instincts began to cloud her mind. So she wouldn't let herself enjoy.

"Is my pretty mouse jealous? Is that what this is all about?" He seemed thoroughly pleased by the concept, a smirk growing on his ravaged face.

Not jealous. Degraded.

19

———————

That look in her eye made his cock swell even fucking bigger, made it spray her with a gush of precum. Shucking his pants and kicking them out of the way, Caspian demanded she look at just who owned her now.

When lavender eyes ran over his chest, when her pupils grew just a little larger, he purred. "Until you learn how to suck my cock better, mouse, Rosie will do it every day. Sometimes she'll do it in front of you before I fuck you. Sometimes she'll do it while you're fucking Kieran or Toby. I like her mouth and I've paid for it."

The female nodded, expression closed no matter how much slick ran at his call.

"If you're a good girl, I'll let her use her mouth on you."

No nod.

Weighing a breast, Caspian warmed to the idea. "She can suck on these tits while I screw your brains out."

Nothing.

Nipple rolled between forefinger and thumb, a quick tweak and pinch left the flesh pink and inviting. "She can lick your cunt, stretch your ass… get you ready for all the things I want to do to you."

The Omega pushed her legs together, the movement so subtle that had Caspian not been watching closely for a reaction, it would have been missed.

He had found her limit so easily… and what a boring limit it was. "You disappoint me mouse…"

Lavender eyes raised and for a split second he saw right into her thoughts. It wasn't his disappointment that inspired his visceral reaction in that moment, it was hers. *She was disappointed in him.*

The resulting prickly sensation in his bones twinged and twisted. It made demands. Caspian even fucking offered a deep, comforting purr before he could stop himself.

White lashes drooped at the sound, but that unwelcome burn didn't fully wash away.

"Turn around." He couldn't take those eyes on him again. But he could take everything else.

She obeyed.

"Put your hands against the wall." This was more natural: his command, a female's obedience. "Wider, pretty mouse. Now your legs, step them apart and let me see how wet my good girl is for me."

When sweet thighs parted, a little river of slick rushed down her thighs. Proof that no matter her brooding looks, she desired him.

Delving into wet folds with searching fingers, Caspian found no mark of damage from Toby's order to prepare her.

"Did you take all of Toby's fist? Were you a good girl for my Third?"

White hair danced at her lower back when his trapped mouse nodded.

"Did you like it?"

Her hesitation was not of the nature of the ones before. It was contemplative, the following shrug unsure.

There *was* a bad girl in there. One who would learn the thrill of the things Caspian tempted her with. "Did you think of me when you came? Of Kieran? Whose knot did you imagine stretching this pussy?"

The question startled her. Caspian could almost see the mouse's ears pricking—recognized the shift in her scent. Interesting…

Teasing slick-drenched fingers up and down her fluttering slit, he found himself pressed to her back, nose in her hair. When he growled, when his demand shook from his chest, he wanted her whole damn body to feel it. "Did you think of that first time I held you down and took everything you weren't ready to give? How I own you now?" He plunged in two twisting digits, relishing her gasp as he finger fucked through all that seeping fluid. Loud squelching filthy noises filled the air, more delicious cries coming from the bad, bad girl he'd was going to teach her to be. "Did you think of your Alpha's cock? Did you want my cum filling up this sweet cunt?"

The scent of Omega desire grew so thick in the air Caspian was drunk on it. She might play the innocent virgin, but the body pressing back against him was willing no matter the hesitations of the mind.

Breathing heavy at her ear, he swore. "I'll fuck you so hard no other will ever compare."

Fisting his cock, he lined up before she might brace, and shoved forward with such might her body hit the wall. Looking down at the trapped mouse, how her cheek was squished to the paint, how her eyes rolled and twitched, he savaged her hole.

He didn't give her time to adjust to him, but forced everything he had in her belly.

He didn't care if she yelped or mewled each time his sack slapped her ass.

There was nothing of thought when a cunt that tight rippled and spasmed and tempted him to conquer it. He was beyond rough. More than primal.

Those eyes owed him, and so Caspian rooted his fingers into her hair. Yanking back her head, licking at her mouth, he found the lavender gone.

Only black with the thinnest hint of an almost burgundy limbal ring. Eyes that were blank of anything but pleasure.

He'd fuck that out of her too. He'd fuck out the shy, abandoned thing keeping house in the Warrens. He'd fuck out the ferocious protector to two worthless boys. He'd fuck out the resistant, immaculate, pretty mouse who looked so fucking good clean he'd almost kissed her at his door.

He'd fuck this creature into nothingness.

Destroy her.

Make her pay for existing in a world that didn't revolve around him.

Drinking of her lips, high on her cries, Caspian gave over to the rage.

She'd *dared* look at him and found him wanting when he'd found her flawless. Her tight, wet sleeve of flesh that tried to milk at his cock *dared* to quiver and tempt this mating to end.

The fucking smell of her *dared* to incite feelings beyond victory and fire.

"Fucking slut!"

The roar shook out of his massive chest, rolling off the ceiling. Vibrating, every nerve alive with possession, he let slip a bellow.

A single, male call no woman before had earned.

If two other contenders had not opened the door, things might have gone too far.

Caspian might have done more than drag his teeth to her shoulder and pinched the flesh.

He might have torn into her, just as he'd torn into her cunt.

Snarling, all animal, Caspian pulled his mouth from female flesh, snapping his teeth at the intruders. Boxing in his Omega with arms bulging, ready to strike should another male take one step closer, he growled.

"That's what I'm talking about. Fuck her. Fuck her like the slut she is…" Eyes wild to find the barbarism of Caspian pounding the female, his Second wasted no time. Pants open, shirt yanked up, Kieran furiously began to jack off as he stood a wise distance away.

Toby, his beastly exposed dick hanging heavy and swollen, dripped precum on the floor. Eyes glazed, he muttered to himself, "…I get her third."

First-Alpha got first claim. No other male would taste his mouse unless they tasted him on her. That thought, the knowledge that his cum would lace every kiss the Second and

Third might suck from her lips, the way she squealed when he redoubled his efforts and began to rumble with the coming pulse of an epic building knot, sent Caspian over the edge.

He was supposed to knot outside her and ease it into her pussy as it grew… that was the plan so that she might stretch and be ready for Toby later. But it was too late, his knot burst forth and locked tight behind her pubic bone. Balls heavy with unspent sperm drew up and ached with need to expel.

Omega cunt seized, coughing around him in a bid to seat his throbbing meat deeper. He was there, right on target when that the first mighty spray spewed forth to froth and churn in her relentless pulsating grasp.

Internal muscles sucked him for more, mangling his relentless knot in a grip of iron, and left the female wailing in the violence of her release.

"Turn her so I can see." Breathy words, bent with short grunts of pleasure came from

Kieran. "I want to see her hole stretched around you. I want to watch her cunt leak."

To show off his conquest to the pack, to let them observe just what he owned, drew another thick wave of cum straight up Caspian's shaft.

Hand wrapping the front of her throat, First-Alpha displayed his trophy.

Her feet could not reach the floor, not hung as she was on his cock. She dangled, pale legs pathetically kicking in a bid for support.

Kieran stroked himself faster, one thumb rubbing circles over his weeping crown. "God damn… look at that pussy. Stuffed fucking full. I bet you a thousand credits she'll piss herself if you press down."

Toby groaned, face one of twisted pleasure and misery, as his cock dumped sperm on the floor. He had not so much as stroked that thing—would not touch it until his turn— and still he spilled. "Let me taste."

No. He wanted her muscles surging and

struggling to handle his knot, not emptying her bladder and lessening the pressure. "Both of you come here and lick her. She comes the entire duration of my knot or neither of you will get a turn today.

Toby had already fallen to his knees before his First, tongue lashing its way up the girl's leg. Kieran was at his side a second later, flick, flick, flicking a swollen clit.

Noises unlike any he'd heard from a female came from the mute one.

Music, her song… and Caspian came again.

The Omega's legs were propped on his subordinate's shoulders. Watching his two pack brothers fight over who might lick what, feeling her strain her body as if she might actually escape the attention of three males, it was perfection.

20

———————

Wren knew they'd somehow ended up on the bed. She knew the one who'd knotted her had hooked her legs over his forearms and kept her obscenely spread for his men. She didn't know how to make them stop.

Her back sticking to Caspian's sweaty chest and torso, the scrub of his coarse hair scratching overexcited flesh as she relentlessly squirmed, she wordlessly begged.

One fist caught in Kieran's hair, another pushing Toby's bald head away, a surging cramp stole from her womb. The knot Caspian's rocking hips still manipulated inside her didn't shrink in the slightest.

It fucking grew.

She could see where his cock bulged out her belly, could feel the swimming despoilment gushing behind that knot. No matter how she squeezed him, no matter how many times he came, nothing gave.

It was indecent how the two crouched between her legs and lapped up the trickling feast. Toby took it a step further, wedging his arm under her lower back, and angled his hand down between her cheeks. Without any way of avoiding his probing fingers, she'd been left pierced through another hole. Her slick eased his teasing, the stinging stretch as he pulsed in and out of her ass somehow making her orgasms all the more staggering.

"Ungh... make her do that again." The man arching under her threw back his head, cock kicking in the swirling mess of her insides. "Fuck her ass with your fingers. As many as she can take."

Two. Two was all it took before she hissed in pain and the relentless pleasure began to ebb. She almost wished he would have shoved in three and obliterated any last trace of their power over her body.

Kieran ran his hands over her more sensitive ridges, sitting back to watch as he strummed her nub. Their eyes met. The way he licked his lips, how full they'd grown feasting on her clit, left her aching from more than just too much attention.

The base, lower part of herself these males had drawn out felt a surge of vanity in immodesty. Green eyes looked at her with true appreciation. They looked at her with longing.

And deep, *deep* down, there was a very real thrill knowing it was *her* who'd earned that gaze.

Before she could make peace with such an awful thought, he fell on her clit again and the fresh rasp of tongue was too much. Those burning green eyes that silently demanded she watch everything he did to her, blew the last trace of her cognizance away.

Wren came screaming—a long, lingering pull of her pussy wrapping the jerking meat inside her.

She came so fully that the knot that refused to budge was forced an inch lower to crown at the mouth of her cunt.

Beneath her, Caspian howled, bucking to fight his way back in.

Toby shouted, "Let her do it! Get her ready for me!" Eyes wide as he grinned at what brought forth a horrible sting.

Another stomach-clenching surge and his knot was caught at the gate where pink flesh thinned in an effort to ease his exit.

"No you don't!" The subordinate males were kicked back, Caspian rolling Wren to her stomach so he might bear his weight down against her attempt to expel him. Driving his way through taut muscles and over-full cunt, he reseated his knot just as another wave of boiling cum burst forth. Breathing heavy, he rocked his hips, grunting at her ear, "Be a good girl and hold this fucking knot until I'm done with you."

Upon hearing his growl, his pleasure, her insides obeyed, sucking him even deeper than he had been before.

Without the constant stimulation of the other two males, it was bearable. Pleasurable to focus only on the pulse and beat of the male flesh inside her.

Flattened under the weight of a beast, one who began to purr when she began to pant in relief, Wren closed her eyes to all of it.

The body endured but the mind flew far away. By the time he finally slopped his last possible spend against her womb, she was in tune with something greater than herself.

The knot began to subside.

Pressure released with a pop.

Wren couldn't see who, but she felt a mouth gobbling up what ushered forth.

Toby…

It was Toby. Kieran was too busy fisting his cock on the bed beside her. Hand a blur of motion, he came on her face, a sticky spider web of semen stretching from her check to chin.

A hungry groan came from the bald head that butted her thighs apart in a bid to get more, and Caspian's knot shrunk.

Another wave of fluids rushed out to soak the bedding.

Eyelids drooping, the grunts and groans of three men filling the air, Wren fell asleep.

DRAWING out of her fluttering sheath, Caspian ground his teeth on a groan. The rasp of over-stimulation against his cock both stung and enticed, and if he didn't leave her saturated cunt, he was going to fuck his mouse a second time.

The temptation, the rattling whir of her

sleepy purr, it made it impossible to share with the two males already reaching for her.

Caspian dropped his head to scent her neck and calm himself… he'd never taken it that far with the other girls. Not to the point the female had passed out cold.

He'd never fucked an Omega while simultaneously threatening his pack. He'd never once been territorial over cunt.

Drawing in a rib-stretching breath, he reminded himself that there was nothing special about this girl. She was just a good lay. Best goddamn pussy he'd ever had.

An Omega who didn't know her place. Who had challenged him.

One who had dared push him away.

His cock began to ache just thinking of how good it had felt to fuck her up against the wall. To know there would be bruises that *he* put on her. Punishment served.

She might have said no, might have insulted him with those eyes, but no other cunt screamed *yes* like hers did. And since an inexperienced castoff like her was incapable of faking a single smile or moan, her every last cry had been genuine.

For him.

For his cock.

His cum.

His brutality.

She'd liked being battered against the wall. And though it might have shocked her ridiculous virginal sensibilities, Caspian had felt how hard her pussy squeezed him when she realized Kieran and Toby—his pack—had come in to watch.

Her devious little pussy was greedy for sperm, always trying to urge the knot out of him after the first thrust.

Cum slut.

His cum slut, for now. And she'd get plenty tonight by the time Kieran and Toby had their fun. She'd be marched back to her room, jizz dripping from every last pore, leaving a splattered trail for his gang to sniff at when they walked the halls. She'd wake up tomorrow with no fucking clue what happened to her, why she'd wanted it, why she was going to grow addicted.

Naive Omega… a pretty, mute mouse. He'd make sure she craved him. That she'd learn to patiently wait while Rosie sucked his cock and took the edge off.

He'd make her watch next time. The Omega lying back on this very bed with her legs spread so that as she grew aroused, she'd be unable to hide it. From him or herself.

Under him, the mouse's purr-laced snores rattled on. The sound was… unhealthy… and stole his attention away from the fantasy. The source of his consternation clattered out a congested hum—and for the first time, he *listened* to it.

He hated the weak, sick sound as much as he thirsted for it.

Looking down at his sleeping prize, Caspian eyed the globs of Kieran's cum splattering her face and scowled.

When his Second haltingly reached forward to rub his scent into her skin, contact was not allowed. Without thought, Caspian grabbed the other Alpha's wrist, warning him off with a snarl.

"Tonight's for pack." Kieran lowered down, challenging in stance yet placating in tone. "Tonight we share and grow stronger for it."

The burgeoning growl vibrating from an aggressive First-Alpha's throat didn't stutter, Caspian warning, "You'll get your turn when I say you get your turn, Second. Back the fuck off. She's tired."

Kieran lowered his head, but not in submission. He lowered his head ready to charge. "You're still caught in the rut, and I swore to you I wouldn't let you bite her. I'm not going to let you play mate with her either and incite a greater urge. Get off the Omega. Summon Rosie if you need another fuck to take the edge off. Summon the whole fucking pen before you do something we would all regret. Pack *always* comes before cunt."

Another challenge rumbled from a throat tense with twitching muscle. "You will have your turn when I say it's your turn. The Omega needs rest, water, and something sweet... unless you want to fuck a ragdoll. Back the fuck off until I say you can touch her."

"You want to build her a fucking nest next? She's a whore who sold herself for spoils like all bitches do."

Toby had his own complaints. The huge throbbing *thing* that had once been a dick dragged over saturated covers, the Third challenging for the girl. "I'm going to fuck her tonight, Caspian, even if I have to rip your goddamn head off! I like this one and I've waited."

His Third *had* been forced to wait. He'd been given assurances. And with his balls and cock swollen like they were, there was good reason he lacked the capacity to be patient. But his Second... it was not like Kieran to challenge. He'd seen what had happened to the last Second who'd thought to command his first.

He'd also been the first male Caspian had mounted after the fight had been won. He'd fucked him dry, just like he'd fucked Toby dry—to establish rank and show the other, dangerous males, who ruled The Syndicate.

He'd fuck him right now if Kieran didn't watch his goddamn mouth.

"She's just a girl, Caspian. You're blinded by the rut… it's not worth risking pack. Not over something already agreed upon between us all."

The white-haired female stirred, settling herself deeper into the covers, a little tongue darting out to taste her cum-globbed lips. That hadn't been his cum that had put a sleepy smile on her mouth after a single lick.

Her shoulders weren't marked by a bleeding bite that said she was his.

This *was* just a girl.

Slowly, the angry fog cleared, Caspian blinking hard. He was in the wrong here and was man enough to admit it. Weight shifting, Caspian rolled to pant at the drowsing mouse's side. Throwing an arm over his eyes, he pushed until he saw stars. Until his vision matched his sparking insides.

Any minute now, he'd burst out of his skin, a true case of spontaneous combustion.

Any minute now, he'd kill the two faithful Alphas who helped him run The Syndicate.

For what? A defective female who couldn't speak and dared judge his tastes?

Fuck her.

Concessions had to be made to his men. "Do whatever you want to her. Anything."

"Anything?" Toby edged nearer, wasting no time laying hands on the Omega. Flipping her to her back and spreading her thighs wide, he licked his lips and prepared to devour the viscous, milky seepage from her slit. "Anything I want?"

Already pawing her face to rub his spend into her skin, Kieran snarked, "Don't kill her."

"Fuck you, Kieran. I told you that was an accident."

"Yeah, keep telling yourself that." Handsome, mean grin in place, the Second looked pointedly at Toby's gnarled, knot-swollen cock. "You take things too far."

"They were Betas. This is an Omega. She's built for what I can give her."

A lower, much more vicious snarl came from the Alpha lying back and trying to gather himself. Lowering his arm from his eyes, he locked them both in a dead stare before speaking. "I am in no mood to hear you two bickering. Fuck the Omega and get out."

Without another word, Toby fell on the female to suck whatever he could get from her womb. When she gave a disquiet groan in her sleep, it was the Second who threw him off. "It's not your turn! Go play with your mangled dick, and get the fuck outta my way. You want to swallow globs of cum, suck off Caspian."

They all knew it wasn't cum he was after.

Toby was an addict. Slick was his drug of choice… slick laced with his leader's spend something he craved as Third.

The sheer fact that Caspian's hard-on was slippery with the mouse's juices was the only reason the male crept between his annoyed leader's spread thighs and began to lick the man from base to tip. When that no longer tasted of female, Toby let his tongue drag over the First Alpha's saturated sack.

It appeased Caspian, who grew less possessive of a disposable Omega and more focused on selfish pleasure. It also gave Kieran something to watch while the female was still out cold.

Stroking his cock, he let Toby bathe him with his tongue, rubbing out a quick orgasm that dribbled out the sad leftovers from spent testes. When the Third pulled back and scowled at the slow white drips, moving down a veined cock like candle wax, Caspian used the moment to establish dominance and remind him who ran the show. "Lick that off. Swallow it, Toby."

Kieran didn't prefer males, but Caspian knew his Second got a thrill watching any time Toby was made to submit. Curved cock in his hand, Kieran stroked and stared, just about ready to blow.

When Toby wrapped his lips around his First-Alpha's cock, Caspian made sure their eyes met. "And when Kieran cums, you'll suck that down too. Consider this a light reprimand. Next time you threaten to rip my head off, I'll fucking kill you."

21

Caspian was in a mood, and his mood spilled over onto the rest of them. Agitated, Kieran watched his friend watch him, and fought the low, building growl he so wanted to spit in the First-Alpha's face.

It was *his* turn, and the First had said *anything*.

Kieran's anything started now.

Slipping his arms under the sleeping female's body, he lifted the slight thing to his chest, and moved her to the opposite edge of the bed. It was better she was away from the First considering their leader's minor obsession with this new toy.

Get her away before some fucked up instinct told Caspian to interfere the second she made a squeak of pain.

After all, she wasn't going to like taking a cock up her ass for the first time. Omegas never did. It went against their natures and almost always led to tears. But she needed to be punished for causing this tension between them, and Kieran needed to claim some untouched part of her for himself.

Break her in.

Set the precedent now, so that when all three of them fucked her at the same time, she wouldn't squeal when both holes were used at once.

That's what was needed to ease this mood. A mutual fuck. Three Alphas taking their pleasure in unison.

But not tonight. Tonight they each were to have their turn.

Looking down at the dazed woman, he could see that she'd begun to rouse. Good. Toby was the sort to fuck a ragdoll; Kieran wanted his woman aware, participating even if she hated it.

After all, they'd made a deal. What fun was there in collecting if he didn't get to enjoy the coming shock on her face when his dick slid home?

Or the glory of bulging eyes when her ass started to fill up with ropes of cum. He'd make her hold it in when he pulled out, watch as she shimmied off the bed to make it to the toilet before humiliating herself. A spermy enema that was a bit cruel considering he knew the cramp that came when all that fluid shot up where the sun don't shine.

But there was no better way for an Alpha to establish dominance, and this little girl blinking up at him needed to learn her place.

Reaching down, he gave her an arbitrary caress. Not sure why he allowed his palm to skim her belly, or why he met her eyes and let a lingering, kneading grip warm her hip. "It hurts less if you don't fight. Submit and I'll go easy on you."

She didn't understand, the bob of her throat as she swallowed, the widening of her eyes, displaying anxiety and confusion. Kieran dragged his touch to her knees, bringing them up to her shoulders and commanding the Omega to, "Hold yourself open for me."

Red-faced, she obeyed, every cum smeared inch of pussy and ass on display. Compressed as she was, a slow moving slop of slick continuously poured from her slit to coat her anus. It lubricated his fingers, Kieran finding that Toby had stretched her enough that one digit slid in with little resistance.

Now was the moment of truth, that brief, shocking understanding dawning on the

Omega's face. White lash-framed eyes widened at the intrusion, the female stretching up as if to displace him. Using all that slippery fluid, he withdrew the single digit and replaced it with three.

The burn made her face screw up and the subsequent clench left her pussy coughing more spent cum out to drip over his probing fingers.

Their eyes met, Kieran unblinking as he watched the subtle play of pain on her face.

Toby scooted closer, unwelcome when he leaned down to stroke her forehead. "Relax and take deep breaths, sunshine. He isn't going to damage you. In time, you'll even learn to like it."

The Third's soliloquy stole lavender eyes from glittering green, and left Kieran bristling toward the purring male. "Look but don't touch, Toby. You'll get your turn when I'm done. Right now she's mine and I don't feel like sharing."

Might as well have been the motto of the evening.

Stretching that tight ring, Kieran began to scissor his fingers. It was less to give her pleasure and more to get this over with. Rosie had sucked him off in the hall, Kieran had already jacked off watching Caspian knot her brains out, and then again watching Toby lick their leader… perhaps that was why every time she let out a little grunt of pain or jerked, his cock got softer.

He wasn't enjoying this as he should have been. Scowling, using his free hand to rub some life back into this dick, he worked her ass all the harder.

Toby no longer touched, but he continued to say sweet things to her, would purr for her.

Already smitten.

By the end of the night, the Omega would want nothing to do with the Third, no matter how much he might fawn, pet, or grin.

Let him whisper encouragement now if it

mean Kieran's dick would be seated all the sooner.

After all, the Omega should be grateful Kieran only wanted her ass. She should be thanking him. Licking her lips. Begging for his attention.

She should learn to smile at him like all the other whores did.

Across the bed, Caspian kept his distance, even when Kieran jammed his fingers too far and a pained yelp fell from pretty, parted lips. Watching from the other side of his expansive bed, he didn't even offer a purr. Instead, it seemed as if the First's muscles rippled in time to Kieran's thrusting, wriggling fingers.

He couldn't complain about losing the right to fuck her ass first. He'd said *anything*.

Whipping his hand out of her stretched hole, Kieran thrust his flagging dick into her dripping cunt, displaced more of Caspian's cum, and lubed up. Four hard, yet slowly paced thrusts, shook the sprawled body, the

Omega's tits bouncing, her mouth open and sucking in air in time with his assault.

The velvet feel of her around him brought blood pounding back into aching meat, left a tingle growing in his balls, and encouraged a feral grin to thin his lips. One thrust he was in her cunt, and the next he'd lined up with a different hole.

He went in harder than he should have… and it was glorious.

All of her clenched in a way pussy never could, trying to push him out instead of sucking him deeper. Catching her legs to his shoulders, he fell on her and humped like a teen riding his first hooker. If she was screaming, or crying, or making any sort of racket, he didn't care. Eyes shut tight, he pushed and pushed until that passage gripped every last inch of his cock.

Which was fully hard, and throbbing out a heartbeat in her bowels.

More of her scent invaded his nose, the smell of woman, of soft purrs and sweet smiles. Eyes screwed shut, he imagined her that way while ransacking a part of her no Omega wanted to give.

Domination. This was so much more. Hips swiveled side to side between thrusts, back bent so he could cocoon all around her.

This was ownership.

She was property. His property.

She would play his games, nest in the bed they shared—smile and kiss and let him destroy her ass. As if she wanted him.

Groaning, ratcheting up his pace, he found her mouth and owned that too. And still he kept his eyes closed. Building pressure in the balls slapping her ass left sensation twisting at the base of his spine. The whole of him inside her kicked, expanding as that first burst of cum began to spew.

The beginning of the knot was tucked behind her sphincter. Pulling back before he tore delicate skin, he groaned. That tight clutch of skin almost didn't give, but when it did, he heard her for the first time since it began.

She moaned.

Not in pleasure…

In the bearing of something despised.

Ready to punish her for refusing to like him, Kieran pulled back his hips. Just before he snapped forward to force her to take the knot, consequences be damned, Toby wrapped a tight grip around the expanding knot and tricked his body into dumping out the heaviest rush yet.

Caught up as he was, Kieran hadn't even noticed the rival male had come up behind him. Locked in his arms, both of the Third's hands gripping and pulsating and mimicking Omega cunt, his subordinate milked his cock the way an asshole never could.

He filled her up with every ounce of cum Kieran had left.

All the while, Kieran stared into lavender eyes. Whatever she saw in his expression as orgasm devastated its way through his senses, left her to reach out a hand and lightly pat his shoulder.

Even as her inevitable internal cramping grew from all the fluid he shot deep, she caressed that spot. Soothing the troubled beast.

In an uncharacteristic act of magnanimity, the urge to show her there could be more moved his hand lower. He found her clit, and touched her with all the gentleness his cock had denied her. Stuffing her ass full, whispering the same tender words of encouragement Toby had muttered, Kieran began to purr. "There is pleasure in this if you let go and submit. I know it hurts now, but cum for me, and learn to relish the pain."

Not a speck of trust was in those violet eyes. There couldn't be when something so vulnerable had been used so callously. A man who watched everything, who could read a person with a single look saw…

…how lonely she was. How even surrounded by three of the most powerful Alphas in Dale City, she felt unsafe.

As if trying to justify this, Kieran increased the pressure on her clit. "We treat the females in the pen good."

The female gave an obligatory nod, breathing through the discomfort and what had to be an overwhelming urge to empty her bowels.

"I'll pull out and help you to the bathroom, but not until you cum."

Her eyes begged, and they begged beautifully.

"You can do this." He pulsed where he corked her, offering a single growl to stimulate where he teased. "Can't you, pretty girl? Can't you cum for me?"

The seductive drawl of an Alpha purr-laced order began to work its magic. Kieran could smell it on her, smell the arousal despite the discomfort. Another growl rumbled past his lips, loud and hungry. He poured that noise over her trembling limbs, into her body, and drew out the tiniest mewl when she unwittingly obeyed.

It wasn't an obliterating orgasm, but it was enough to take the edge off.

Half her tension melted away.

"I'm going to pull out." Giving her an approving smile, he took ahold of the base of his cock, slowly working his way out. "Hold it all in. Can you do that for me? Can you keep all of my cum inside this beautiful ass? I'll help you get up, and I'll take care of you."

22

Caspian had pounded her into a blubbering mess against the wall, then held her open like a prize kill for his pack to feast on. The dominant Alpha with red lipstick smeared on his chest had ordered his men to force orgasm after orgasm until pleasure burned each nerve and left her gasping in fizzling shocks instead of rapture.

She'd been made to tolerate two tongues rasping a throbbing clit. Nibbling teeth marking her thighs. The looks in the eyes of the males.

Possession, desire, impatience…

Yet when it was over, she had not been treated with the care an Alpha should show. No water, no real rest.

She was here to serve and play a role. And somehow she'd already disappointed them.

Kieran hadn't given a shit for her comfort, seeking his own in her pain. His weight had offered no safety, he had given no purr.

Wren wasn't as naive as these men seemed to think. She knew some males took their pleasure in unnatural ways. It had been awful, completely uncomfortable, but she'd endured. There had even been a moment near the end where it wasn't all bad, and something about that had been worse than the initial discomfort.

She didn't want to enjoy—and both males in very different ways had reduced her to some animal state where a bone-deep gratification was found in their evils. Their lie of coupling.

They made her truly *defective*.

Good men did not treat their females like this.

Damaged men drunk on power did.

Good men pulled frightened girls out of the mud they were dropped in. They took them in, sheltered them, taught them to forage, and learned their silent language.

Wren had known a good man once.

A man who had never tried to touch her without permission.

A man who was gone and who would never come back.

She'd been unable to give him... *this*. But if she had, she would have done any of these depraved acts with all her heart if it would have pleased him half as much as Kieran watching her release her bowels had.

Caspian's Second had cooed and pet her, a completely different man as she cramped in humiliation and spilled. Kissing her forehead, he'd called her a *good girl*, the context very different than when Caspian spoke the same words.

He had put her in an honest-to-god shower when it was over and washed her head to toe, purring so loudly she was unable to push him away like she should have.

Starved for comfort, she had accepted it from the worst of them.

She'd even cried on his chest, and clung to him as precious *warm* water rushed over the various stings and hurts. She'd drunk the rivulets running over his hairless chest, rubbed her face against skin that held to the fragrant lie of safety.

Held by the Second, Wren had fallen apart.

A man she didn't like slowly put her back together.

How the women here survived the mind-fuck, she'd never know. It was so much more damaging than anything physical they might do to her body. The offering of a dedicated

Alpha to a tired, run down Omega in need of succor was cracking her mind.

There were moments where it almost felt honest, where she felt a connection. And it was a lie.

Wren had not forgotten about the red lipstick smeared over Caspian's heart. She'd never forget the way Kieran had layered anger and threats in his viciousness on the bed.

And Toby, he appeared sweet and accommodating, but there was something in his smile that spoke of a man holding on to sanity by a thread.

Three worse males could not exist.

At least the Alpha who'd torn her maidenhead had been clear in his intentions. These Alphas were anything but.

When even warm water would not stop her shaking, Kieran made assurances, "You need to eat something, sweet thing. That's all this is."

No, it wasn't *all this was.*

"I'll give you a hit of the good stuff for the pain. It will make the rest of the night…" Even Kieran couldn't tell that lie.

She shook her head. She'd seen firsthand what The Syndicate's drugs could do.

The other males invaded Caspian's bathroom, watching from the door, though they might as well have been skin to skin with her. She could feel them real enough, smell their various scent-markers, hear their purrs or lack thereof.

Her break was over.

After swallowing all the water she could hold, rinsed of foulness, Wren pulled her arms from the *thing* that had been holding her up. She stepped away from the purring Alpha and did not meet his eyes as she signed. *"Let's get this over with."*

Ever interested, Toby asked, "What does that mean?"

It meant that she wanted to see Mikael and that she still had to let Toby put his very swollen organ into her body. Fighting the shakes, she used the alphabet she'd taught him earlier, slowly spelling out. *"Your turn."*

He sounded it out, letter by letter, grinning from ear to ear when understanding struck home. "Step away from Kieran and come to me. Come be all mine, sunshine."

Naked, wet, bruised, and sore, Wren forced a smile and put on the show Kieran had demanded in exchange to see her boy. She abandoned the suddenly grumbling Alpha in the shower. Ignored the looming largeness of their spying leader, and padded across the floor to present herself to Toby.

The air grew ripe with the musk of thrilled male.

Purring, projecting soothing vibration both raw and rich, Toby pulled off his shirt.

It was the first time he'd disrobed before her.

The Third was just as well-muscled as the other males, but covered in dye saturated flesh common on gangsters. Tattoos, some well-drawn, some old, faded, and from another era marked his chest and arms. When her attention ran over his art, he displayed, posturing with a great deal of enthusiasm.

Scars, there were so many scars under the ink: bullet wounds, gashes, *tallies*.

This freakish man had saved her special dress… twice.

He had also shoved a fist into her body only this morning.

Eyes caught on the throbbing monstrosity hanging like a gnarled tree branch between his legs, Wren bit her lip. It twitched under her gaze, jumping as if already seeking out the sleeve that would end its pain.

She should not have thought of it as something that was alive, but it *looked* alive with all those pulsating veins and a drip, drip, dripping head—a salivating alien slug ready to burrow and eat her from the inside out.

"I want you to scent me." He trailed his fingers from a ripped chest to a meaty neck. "Here. Take all the time you need. When you're ready, take my hand. Together we'll build a nest and share it properly. I won't force you against the wall or on an unprepared bed. Give me a chance to respect the communion." Reaching out, fingers carded through her dripping hair. "I know something special when I see it."

Everything he said seemed like the perfect speech an Alpha might make when presented with a bride, but Wren had heard enough in simple banter between these males to know that Toby had no idea how to *respect the communion.*

If he did, he would not have done *that* to his genitals, or been eager to inflict it on her.

"You want her to build a nest on *my* bed to fuck *you* in it?" Caspian was not at all pleased, rumbling a warning as he staunchly refused to purr.

"You said *anything.*" Brows dropping over her ice-cold eyes, Toby turned, put himself between Wren and the First. "I want to nest with her."

"You know what happens when you nest."

Reaching back to nudge his knuckles under Wren's chin, Toby smirked as if thrilled by the idea. "I get attached."

That was far more terrifying than his raging, deformed hard-on.

Scowl becoming a frown, Toby sniffed the air over Wren's head before snarling at Caspian. "You frightened her! Boss, we had an agreement."

Unmoved, like a fucking wall of stone, Caspian, the male who publicly wore a coat made out of people stated, "She should be frightened. You're a fucking mental case who gets his kicks in interrogation and torture. I saw you cum cutting off Gizzard's feet a week ago. Play house, but don't mislead the mouse. You're no prince charming, and the Warrens rat isn't going to turn into a queen."

Red anger burned, turning eyes that had been ice to fire. "Nellie had a good life with me!"

"Fuck with all the Betas you want.

Omegas…" Eyes catching on the only Omega in the room, Caspian caught himself, snapping his teeth audibly and thinning his lips.

Omegas what?

"Sir, Toby prepared her just as you ordered." Kieran wrapped a towel around his waist, and came to stand between them. Eyeing the dripping woman holding tight to her middle he said, "Take a trip to the pen and leave them to it. Take out your rut on the girls, not our pack brother. Rosie is real keen on making up with you. Let her try."

Pushing his weight from the door frame, Caspian stalked forward, right up into Toby's equally snarling face. "She better not be damaged when I get back."

No. No. No. No. No. No. Caspian could not leave her alone with this guy. Kieran was intimidating for sure, but if things got out of hand, as he had so kindly hinted they would, she needed a male of Caspian's power and repute to keep her from what might be a terrible death.

"It's okay." Toby rounded on her, finding Wren falling into a panic. "It's okay, sunshine. He's in the rut. He doesn't want to share. That's all it is. I could list off scary shit he's done too; same with Kieran. You enjoyed accepting both of them. You'll enjoy being with me too."

She had not enjoyed Kieran, and she had been reduced to a mindless slavering animal when Caspian had played his games.

Slipping around Toby before he could get a good grip on wet flesh, Wren made a grab for Caspian's hand.

Eyes wide with meaning, chest rising and falling and rattling out a broken purr to entice, Wren held on and dug in her feet.

Stay.

"What do you think you're doing?"

Laying her ear atop the red stain on his chest, she enticed the only way that she could. It wasn't even worth feeling disgrace in this act. She knew exactly how degrading this was.

Lacing her fingers with his, feeling his disinterest in holding her hand, Wren gently tried to lead him from the room. He did follow, but not in good spirits. He followed, vibrating with warning her that imminent punishment would be had for this. Still, she got him to his chair, and urged him to sit.

Hands to his chest, she leveled the snarling male with a look that said, *please stay*. She pet him in the way she'd come to learn he enjoyed, ignoring the sound of breaking things and roaring from the bathroom.

"It was MY TURN!"

"Calm down, Toby. I'll drag her back in here and hold her down for you if I have to."

Patting Caspian's chest, urging him to stay just so, Wren took a deep breath. On the exhale, she left the First-Alpha and walked back to the bathroom to find Toby attacking anything he could get his hands on.

Shelves had been ripped off the walls, sundry items crushed. Chaos abounded.

He looked every bit as insane as she'd suspected he was, and it was adrenaline alone that kept her moving forward. When he side-eyed her, snorting like a raging bull, she forced a shy smile and held out her hand.

23

———————

A hair's breadth away from breathing fire, Toby stalked through his carnage—one eye dilated fully, the other stuck and somewhat twitching. He snorted, muscles in his neck jumping while the male rattled like a pissed-off snake.

The female dared return.

Slight, her teeth knocking together. Pretty lips shaped into a smile.

A lie.

It reeked of fear. They *always* reeked of fear.

Her little, bare feet padded over broken bits of jagged-edged debris until the soft tinge of Omega blood seasoned the air just enough for his nostrils to twitch.

She'd hurt herself to come to him.

Good.

Let her get on her knees and beg after blatant rejection, and maybe she'd live through the night.

But she didn't genuflect. Instead the pale, colorless thing put her hands to his chest as if they were intimate, and pressed the cold tip of her nose to his heart. Her loud, nasal inhale left a brain frazzled twinge popping cells in his skull.

Toby stilled… abnormally so.

Not even breath stretched his ribs. The *I'm-going-to-pulverize-every-bone-in-your-pelvis* growl caught mid vibration, when the pretty thing placed an ear to his chest.

The world grew so silent, Toby was sure his beating heart had gone stagnant.

This was death, right there in the form of

an albino beauty. One who had given him the basics of her language only this morning. Him. No one else.

She…

She smelled *divine*.

That first deep breath, groaning into her hair, Toby clawed at her flank and snapped her flush to his body. Reciprocating, the Omega nosed his neck as she should have at first blush, stroking him with the flutter of an unsure female purr.

Soft fingers sought out the shape of him, tracing over the ridges of muscle that flexed in his arms. She reached higher still to massage the shell of his ears between gentle forefinger and thumb.

No one had ever touched him there, in that way, before. And it felt… wonderful.

He would have sworn he felt the hot salt of tears run down the clenched muscles of his stomach, but when she pulled back and met his eyes, a smile was there.

She signed, one hand cupping his cheek, the other spelling out her invitation.

When I was sold, the mate who rejected me never allowed me to build him a nest.

It took Toby both time and focus to make out what she tried to communicate; each stumbled-over word dragging him back from that abnormal stillness. When the sentence was strung together, he pressed his forehead to hers and rumbled out a deep, "What was his name?"

The way the female cut her glance to the side and grew withdrawn spoke for her. She even put her fingers to the black tattoo on her cheek and made a noise of remembrance.

Toby liked the mark, he liked the intention behind it, and he especially liked this woman.

That mark had saved *her* for *him*.

This female whom he wanted to nest with. This female who had never been given the chance to build one for her mate.

One-hundred percent serious, Toby snarled an offer. "Want me to kill him?"

Eyes the same shade as the violet tea set his mother used to favor, darted back to his. They dilated just a touch, the effect ruined when she… laughed.

A *real* laugh, from a fear-tightened chest.

Grinning, all teeth and ill intentions, Toby felt the banging clamor revved back to life behind his ribs. He took it a step further, the loudest purr of the pack spinning its way out of his bones and into her very naked and extremely appealing body.

Kieran, ever the unwelcome male, gaped from where he dared watch Toby put his hands on the pretty one. The pretty one who had not so much as spared a glance for the cocky, good-looking jackass.

She had come in here for *him*.

Which was perfect because he wanted to keep her.

She understood. He knew it.

That was why she smiled and purred and gave him her undivided attention.

But he'd scared her…

"I could find him." Toby cupped her face and pulled her sweet stare back up to his eyes. "Just give me a name."

Her head shook, but it was not in defiance. He could tell by the soft dip of her eyebrows, that she didn't know it.

"Had you been presented in my house, I would have mated you." Sweeping aside her wet hair, he let his fingers dance on her shoulder. "Marked you here."

Her sweet purr caught, the female burying her face in his chest where she began to shiver. Bending down, he set his teeth to that spot, gnawing just enough to inspire a yelp.

A stronger tinge of fear wafted from her skin.

He'd hardly broken skin. Lapping at only a single well of blood, Toby fisted the biggest knotted erection he'd ever achieved and rubbed the tender length against her belly.

The weeping head caught on the underside of her tits, smearing the woman with the promise of what he could offer.

"Your sweet pussy is going to take it all. You're going to take it, and you're going to like it."

Swollen ridges and throbbing bumps tripped over her soft skin, Toby indulging in the pain, knowing that when release began, it would be hours-long brain-burning pleasure.

He'd get her addicted to him, stretch her in a way no one else could.

Aching bone deep, tied up in the pain of a forced knot, Toby began to make a myriad of promises if she'd just lay back and let him fuck her in a pretty nest she made just for him.

He promised her a fortune if she'd be the first to take it without crying.

But she'd already lost that bet. Tears marked her cheeks, fell from eyes red with apprehension. Though she did still smile.

He could cheer her up.

The female locked in his arms needed care. She needed food, more water, dedicated attention.

He needed to reassure her.

Hitching his arm under her delicious ass, he lifted her off the debris strewn floor. Spread her wide against his stomach, her pussy cupping a quantity of his pulsating shaft in sweet, slippery petals. He almost dropped and mounted her right there when a trickle of warmth escaped from her cunt to burn his over-ripe dick. Instead, he held her all the tighter and began to march out of the bathroom and back into his First-Alpha's den.

He dumped her on the bed that smelled of other males, snaking his tongue into her mouth to twist and taste before he threw himself back and barked, "Build it. I need to fuck."

WITH THREE SPECTATORS, Wren arranged, fluffed, and layered bedding already wet in places with her spent fluids and the enticing smell of three males' cum. She did everything properly, almost forgetting why the abundance of fabric and soft things was not hers to keep. This nest, *her first nest built from scratch for a breeding male*, she was proud of it.

The pacing Alpha who had not stopped circling the bed was going to entertain his pack mates with his diabolical fetish. He would wreck and ravage the designs of her haven, just as he tore into her body

She rubbed her cheek on the best smelling fabric, letting herself enjoy the final moments before bad things came. That was how one survived the Warrens. The moment was all that mattered.

"Are you thinking of me?"

She'd closed her eyes, lost in something simple and soft when Toby sidled nearer, smiling like a ravenous wolf.

Nodding, lying, Wren made sure not to so much as glance to where Caspian still waited, reeking of impatience in his chair. Or to acknowledge that Kieran lurked nearby, edging nearer with each passing minute.

The Second wanted front row seats to his *show*.

This was the best she could do.

The situation was awful, the men were unworthy, but the nest… she'd assembled it imagining another. And it was beautiful.

Any Omega would envy it.

And she would suffer in it.

A finger traced down her spine. "I'll brace her." Kieran was even closer than Wren thought.

Spittle flung from Toby's mouth when he turned to snarl, "And what makes you think I want to share?"

Slippery and smiling like a tempting demon, Kieran cocked a brow. "Come on, man. Let me help her open up for you. I can make it good for you both. I know how you like your sac kneaded. I can show her where to bite when you arch back."

"No." Rising from his chair, an air of infinite impatience hovering around him, Caspian strode forward. "I will hold her."

The edge of a nail dragging up and down her spine stilled, Kieran grumbling, "Who's going to remind Toby of his place if things go too far?"

Caspian came around the bed, licking his lips as he stared at her tits. "You're Second. You fuck Toby. If you're half as rough with him as you were with her, he'll get the message loud and clear."

Snarling at Kieran, Toby turned on his friend. "You try to stick your cock up my ass, and I'll fucking cut your throat while you're sleeping."

The handsome male ignored the Third's threat, cocking an incredulous brow at Caspian. "You almost sound as if you think I was too rough with her."

"You *were*." In the middle of three males,

Wren kept her eyes on the nest and proceeded to ignore their squabbles, just as she'd ignore what they were going to do to her. Caspian caught her cheek in his palm, raising her head as if she had a part in their conversation. "The mouse couldn't have had it up the ass before, and now she'll cringe each time I expect it. I didn't bring her here to watch her suffer. I brought her here to watch her sing."

Pretentious, unkind, Kieran snorted. "Then why are you giving her to Toby?"

Not an ounce of softness was in Caspian's expression. No love, no adoration. Only a mild hint of mystification as he spoke to Kieran yet studied her face. "Toby doesn't *want* to hurt her. You *did*."

24

This was not expected.

Brace her. Hold her.

The mental nightmare those words inspired was nothing compared to what unfolded upon the bed.

Braced against the headboard, cocooning her limbs, Caspian *cradled* her. He held her back to his chest, encapsulating her body in warm muscles and gently searching fingers. Purring, he crooned at Wren's ear the nastiest of filth said in the sweetest of tones.

Sluicing through folds that still dripped

his cum even after the shower, pinching and tugging them until her slit was totally exposed to the room, he growled, "Open up that tasty pussy, pretty mouse. I want to feel your juices soak my cock while Toby fucks you silly."

Legs hitched over his forearms, spread so the petals of her sex were open, the very hole Caspian referred to suckled air like a little mouth with each tremor his words inspired. It was lewd. The way both Kieran and Toby hovered close to watch each pulse of her cunt, indecent.

Kieran reached forward as if entranced, dragging his fingers from tender anus to hooded clit, touching her as if the dripping slit before him offered a drug more intoxicating than the shit his men sold to the desperate. "I saw you take Toby's whole fist this morning. Yet you still look so tiny."

Two fingers penetrated knuckle deep, Kieran flipping palm upward to seek out something at the roof of her canal—something that made Wren jump and gasp when firm pressure was applied. Stiff, unyielding circles on that spot and her clit swelled to peek out past her hood. Pink, shined tight skin twitched like a beacon to be stimulated, flicked, bit, *anything*.

Anxious, electric shocks tingled under her skin, and two men who knew more about the female body than she did ganged up on her nervous system and sent it into overload. Caspian toyed with her folds, Kieran teased at her cunt, neither of them so much as breathing on her clit.

And it *ached* for attention.

Not that she could ask them to touch her there. Not that she *would*.

Her rolling hips and trembling legs already asked too much.

Wren was eager for this to be over, eager to know why Caspian and Kieran touched her only for her pleasure, and eager for something, *anything*, to be inside her to drive off the gnawing, empty ache.

Pure manipulation. It registered. It did. She knew what this was.

And it was working…

The very atmosphere of the room had changed.

What had been two bickering, dangerous Alphas became three cohesive predators simply because Caspian participated. The unquestioned ruler. The same Caspian who gratuitously praised her when Kieran's attentions drew an unexpected gush of slick to flood his abdomen and run down to soak his balls.

Looking down to where Kieran fingered the internal workings of her cunt, she saw Caspian's dick at full mast. Tall and proud, the helmet-shaped tip beaded with a freshly prepared offering to tempt an Omega.

She could smell him, even with Toby's mangled meat practically pouring out the watery precursor of trapped sperm all over the bedding. She could smell him, and she hated to admit that her mouth watered for a taste.

Another finger poked in, then a fourth.

Unlike the morning, her body opened to the obscene stretch with little more than a few extended pulses. Unlike the morning, it felt…

It felt *nice*.

Again, lavender eyes dragged like an addict toward Caspian's cock. But that was not what Wren was to be given.

No. Toby was on his knees between both her and Caspian's spread thighs, hand lovingly stroking his disfigured cock as if caressing a beloved pet.

Toby and that monstrosity was all she had in store.

But the Third seemed entranced with what his fellow Alphas opened up for him, his attention centered in on her yet untouched clitoris and how it jumped back then swelled forward each time her insides clenched. "Fuck. Fucking cunt's perfect."

Cum still dripped out of her. Caspian had shot so deep that even after being mauled by Kieran, even after a shower, thicker, pearlescent seasoned her slick. It teased the Third, the snarling, completely spellbound psychopath who edged his mouth nearer to where Caspian massaged and pinched her labia and Kieran fucked her with his fingers.

Where her clit was exposed to the air and left buzzing with lack of attention.

Tongue ridged, Toby descended, poking that extended nub and rolling it around as far as the nerve would allow.

The sensation went far deeper, as if linking back down inside to the exact spot Kieran's fingertips rubbed her pussy walls.

Three men, four hands, one mouth, that was what it took to break an Omega.

As if Toby's mouth had gone dry, his rough tongue rasped incessantly. Meanwhile, he sucked that bud between his lips and *pulled*. That was the only way she could describe it. He pulled her spirit right out of the flesh to flail in the ether while the body bucked and died.

Except she breathed, she lived. The heart banging against her chest and the shrill cry a reminder that exquisite torture didn't require the soul's consent.

Clawing at her knees, pulling them wider as if she might pull her enraptured frame in two, Wren threw back her head and found lips waited. Caspian kissed her so deeply, so thoroughly, that her frenzy burst like a bubble of raw magic to explode throughout the room.

She was sobbing when it ended, a mess of tears and runny nose. But she was also completely limp, the only working muscles in her body the pussy that sucked at air with no knot or cock to milk.

The three of them manhandled her supine form into position, Caspian stretching her fleshy labia, Kieran having abandoned her greedy snatch to brace her foot. Toby held the other leg, just as he lifted the weight his mangled dick and notched his weeping head against a girl too weak to refuse… on any level.

"Be my pretty mouse now. Open up for Toby like a good little girl." At the sound of her breathless whimper, Caspian rolled soft lower lips between his fingers and murmured, "That's right. Relax for your Alphas and show us what an eager, willing, and obedient darling you can be. Let Toby in. He's going to fuck your tiny cunt, fill you up so good."

The three of them moved in unison, operated seamlessly in the degradation of one lost female. In that was their power. Alone, each was intimidating, each was to be respected. Yet their true supremacy required Caspian. He kept the bickering Second and Third in line. He made the three of them a single cohesive unit to be feared.

This was how these men ran the waterworks and held every last citizen by the throat. This was why all of Dale City dreaded the reach of The Syndicate.

When in tune, these men were…

Wren had no word for it, she had nothing but the whites of her eyes when Toby began to press the pulsating head of his cock against her flooded slit.

"She's going to do it." Entranced, Toby pulsed where her skin grew pale with a stinging stretch, half that deformed head swallowed by her clenching, clasping channel. "She'll be the first one to take it all."

"Slam it in!" Bracing Wren's leg, Kieran licked his lips, eyes focused and unblinking. "Fuck her until she squeals!"

Bulbous head retreating so her delicate tissue might adjust, Toby adjusted his weight on his heels, brow bunched and temples dotted with sweat. Absently fisting his deformed cock, he ran his hand over the veined, swollen mass that had yet to fit inside, growled, "Sunshine, you gotta let me in now."

Warm hands caressed over her ribs, running upward to cup and tease her breasts. Caspian, the one who held her through this ordeal, the one still kissing her, soothing fear-pricked skin.

He'd never kissed her that way before. Sweetly. Reverently.

Before he only sought to swallow what made her Wren and change the Omega into his eager whore.

Her entrance gave.

With the pop of his glans past her thinned opening, Toby gained ground. And as he did, he let out an animal-deep bleat. Like a bull, snorting, and shaking its head for the stampede, he chuffed, ground his teeth and forced forward into a sheath unprepared for *so much.*

There was no escape by the time that first wave of pain registered. Caspian's grip on her solidified, Kieran rearing up behind the raging bull to brace both her flailing legs wide so Toby's progress would be undeterred.

Toby, who was no longer man. He was all rutting animal, already cumming even though half of his freakish cock had yet burrow into her guts.

And he kept cumming, the fluid that somehow found its way past that hideous cock and her overstretched cunt thick and curdled as it oozed its way out.

The whole length of him was a solid knot, and her body instinctively gripped onto it, muscles grinding down against that monstrous mass… encouraging the raving beast to strain forward until *more and more and more* was fed into her core.

The orgasm that had muddled her senses long enough for Toby to steal in, roared back to life amidst searing pain.

Kieran grinned like a beautiful demon. "Look at her! The slut is going to take the whole fucking thing!"

Flopping like a fish on a hook, Wren seized, eyes rolling back in her skull as the three of them continued with their game.

"*Ahhhhh!*" Trembling, Toby screamed the instant the widest, most mangled part of his cock burrowed home. Locked behind her pubic bone, his overinflated sack drawing up and moving about is if living things wrestled inside it, he flooded her.

Creamy white kept coming, thick enough

to pile up when it splattered Caspian's thighs and stained the bedding.

How the fluid found room to escape the confines of her pussy past that churning, kicking growth, Wren didn't know. She was hardly coherent, trapped in an endless orgasm that would not ease until the entirety of his knot collapsed.

Muscles straining, showing teeth, Toby bumped at her body with jagged, stilted thrusts. He couldn't stop himself, the movement was primal, unavoidable, even horrible.

Because it felt magnificent.

This was why so many tenants of the Warrens were addicted to drugs. This out-of-body feeling of limitless beyond pain.

Sex was never supposed to lead to this place.

Never.

Nirvana belonged to the dead. There would be no coming back from such a thing unchanged.

Pulsating bursts of corrupted bliss deformed her body to shape around that of a very sick man. Toby mutilated her with this knowledge, made her eyes go so far past blown she could see the universe and all its workings.

Limitless. Free of the hideous life she'd lived and the pains she's known, Wren flew.

Hours they were locked together, two bodies warring to fill and be filled. To survive. Hours before Toby was capable of more than mindless grunts so he might mutter two syllables. "Sunshine."

Lucid enough to ruin her world, he made a move the others should have known to watch for.

Toby, the Third Alpha, the unhinged breaker of bodies and enslaver of children, set his teeth to her shoulder and bit down so hard, neither Kieran nor Caspian could pull her free.

25

Hands seized Toby's throat in a death grip, Caspian squeezing, raging to discover the assault only left his Third climaxing even harder. "DO YOU HAVE ANY IDEA WHAT YOU'VE DONE?"

Blood was everywhere, the Omega it spilled from having gone ashen before she'd passed out cold.

Wall-shaking roars bellowed from Caspian's throat. "You fucking tried to bond to her! How dare you!"

Teeth bloody, smile unhinged, the pussy-dazed Third lolled back and chuckled. "Tried? No. It's done. I claimed her."

His mouse was still trapped by Toby's mangled dick, but by the amount of clotted cum that squished out, the freakish knot was finally going down. Still, he could not pull the traitorous male out of her without causing damage she did not deserve. "I'll fucking break your legs, cut you into pieces, and let every slave huddled below piss on your mangled corpse."

Toby smiled all the wider, looking far too contented for a dead man walking. "I watched the surveillance footage. You tried to bite her when she rode your cock on her couch. Instinct told you to set teeth to this one's flesh, yet Kieran held you back. Still you brought her here. Still you want to play. But you don't want *her*, boss. I do. This one."

"Do you think this is some game, boy?" Toby was eccentric, there was no doubt of that, but Caspian was hearing pure madness.

Bonding made an Alpha weak. It made them distracted. It made them vulnerable. "Do you think anyone will respect you now that you bonded? And to a mute no less."

Shaking off drunken listlessness, Toby shoved both his snarling First and hovering Second, shielding the body of the damaged female as if to protect her from *them*. "She's perfect."

Kieran could not have sounded more appalled. "True Alphas resist the call. They breed many."

"Only the stupid ones." Toby's joints began to pop, to crack, muscles swelling as in preparation of battle. "Both of you can fuck who you want. Breed your whole pen. I only want her."

He'd carve Toby apart; remove him from the mouse in pieces if he fucking had to! Panting with fury, ready to rend his Third limb from limb, Caspian bellowed, "SHE WASN'T YOURS TO TAKE!"

The look in his eyes, the cunning flash…

Caspian saw the truth of the matter hidden in the Third's eyes. Toby had thought this through. He'd intended all along to steal his First's newest toy, confirming it when he drew in a deep breath to force the words, "I'll share!" through his wolfish grin.

"You'll share." Dragging out the offensive statement with a raspy growl, Caspian left the bed, the bleeding mouse, and Kieran's disgust behind. He left because the smell of her blood was itching his nose and causing him to salivate. "Do you think that will appease me, Toby? To share something of mine that you *stole*?"

Breaking his silence, Kieran all but ignored the raving Third. Wisely, he turned to his First, met his eye, and announced, "She's not in estrous. Unless reinforced, this bond will be weak. Keep them separated for a few days and she'll have nothing but a scar that could be overtaken by another Alpha."

"No." Like hugging a ragdoll toy to his chest, Toby gathered her close and clung.

"Boss, you told her a few months of riding your cock then you'd set her free. Have your few months with my mate. When you don't want her anymore, she'll nest with me." Throwing a finger toward Kieran, Toby snarled, "And I know what this ignorant fucker has in mind. Breed her then sell her to some stodgy old fucker. It's not going to happen."

"Call me ignorant again, and I'll cut out your goddamn tongue!" Kieran might have had all the beauty a male could ask for, but unlike Toby, he'd had none of the education... He'd never hidden resentment well, and in that moment Caspian could see how it burned him to be mocked for his shit childhood. "Watch yourself, *friend*. I'm not opposed to Caspian's bleeding you dry."

And there it was—the smug arrogance only a highborn patrician of Dale City could wield with such scorn. Toby let it loose: the accent, the air, the roll of his tongue. "You know who my father is. What I bring to the table can't be replaced with *dumb, brute force*, pretty boy, or even fear of The Syndicate's power."

"You might be Governor Ross' spawn, but there are other means to keeping a stranglehold on the Council."

Deranged laughter, even a snort, and Toby said, "Good luck finding a single one of them willing to leave the lap of luxury for the astringent stink of *this* torture chamber. I'm one of a kind, Kieran. I made sure of that when I murdered all my brothers."

Finished watching from the shadows, huge, menacing, and only too happy to smile, Caspian made his threat. "You still have a sister, Toby. A pretty one…"

Eyes going dark, Toby's jaw grew twitchy. "Females are barred from the Council. Even if you took Henriette, even if my pussy of a father continued to bow to your every whim, once the old man dies, you'd lose the seat, you'd lose your spy, and all you'd have is another bitch for your pen."

Hitching a brow, Caspian purred, "You care so little for the pampered miss?"

"I care. But the only way you'd lay a finger on my Etta is if I were dead. Not much I can do from the grave but laugh while your hold on the city slips away..." Rocking the unconscious mouse on his lap, Toby ground his hips against her supine form as he hissed, "There's always someone willing to do what it takes to steal what you got, Caspian. That's why *pack* holds power together. I don't even mind standing as Third—" The man's words caught for a moment, Toby's eyes rolling back on a groan.

Incredulous, Kieran looked down where the mouse was still speared by Toby's enormous cock, scoffing, "Are you... are you still cumming in her?"

"Ummmm...." Toby took a deep, satisfied breath before opening his suddenly sanguine eyes. "Yes. And she's still milking my cock for more."

Kieran just shook his head. "You've got some balls, Toby…"

"She could be your mate too." White hair was carefully pulled back to expose the sleeping woman's other shoulder to the Second. Tempting him with the smooth, unmarked skin. "You could breed her just like you want, get her fat with your baby."

Caspian spoke, but the words were gnarled with grit and broken glass. "Careful, Toby. You can't sell what's mine. And make no mistake about who she belongs to."

He nodded, oddly agreeable. "And when you're done with her, she'll come back to me. After you've grown bored, it should make no difference if I keep her. Fuck, I'll kidnap any bitch you want as a replacement. My gift to you, boss."

No act against the First would go unpunished. Toby would suffer for this. "I want Henrietta."

Lips thinned, Toby's expression vicious,

but his answer was collected and compliant. "Done."

"You'd give us your sister?"

Eyes tracked back to the sickly woman bleeding in his arms. Fingertips brushing at the weeping crescent wounds on the mouse's shoulder, he speculated. "I often wonder if it's really fear that pushes Alphas to reject the call of the bond. All the posturing, all the power, I never found it nearly as satisfying as I do the sight of my mark on her skin. The ultimate taboo. A truly *criminal* thing to do."

Scoffing, Kieran muttered, "Fucking Socrates over here."

Arranging her body so she might rest more comfortably against his chest, Toby drawled, "I'll give you Etta on the same terms you promised our ray of sunshine here. When you're done with her, she goes home—pockets full, enough water for a year."

"Oh…" Caspian crossed his arms over his chest. "That was only the beginning of my demands. You won't be walking out of this room. You'll submit to every last degenerate thing I can imagine. Starting with sucking my cock while you're still inside her. Then Kieran's. You don't even want to know what I intend to do after that."

Brow lowering, eyeing them both as if considering making a challenge, Toby said, "She'll wake up and see it."

Caspian nodded. "Yes, she will. She'll see you bleed far more than she did."

26

―――――

She could not stop the tears. Sobbing, throwing herself over the boy, Wren clung. And wept, and wept, and wept.

Mikael hugged her right back, their various IV cords tangling and pulling where ports had been stabbed into soft flesh.

She'd never seen him as anything but sickly and skeletal. But now, after only a few days in a proper doctor's care, tended in a clean room, *fed*, he almost looked like a regular boy from the upper levels.

Almost.

He was still sick, sicker even than she was, and the doctor had not made her prognoses with a smile. Acute pneumonia that would kill her if not treated immediately. This he'd said after she'd woken from a horrible nightmare filled with screams and pain. This, after coming to in a strange bed, over-bright lights burning her eyes.

There was only one familiar thing in the moment. Watchful, Kieran stood in attendance, scowling from the door.

Already she had been hooked up to machines, various fluids cascading into her veins, a catheter between thighs that ached. The doctor had told her she'd been kept under for three days, that she'd been fed with a tube, and that was why her nostril was sore and crusted with blood. That she had been ordered to follow treatment and he was permitted to sedate her if she attempted to resist.

And she did. She fought back wildly *because she could not pay*.

Of course she wanted to be well. Of

course she wanted to live. But she only had to live long enough for Mikael to get better. If she was dragged off to pay off her debt in the mines, Caspian would throw him out. And her boy would be sick, alone, and have no one to provide for him.

There would be no one there when he inevitably died…

From disease, or hunger, or the unending violence of the Warrens.

It had taken two grown men to hold her down, dour Kieran and the stunned doctor finding the malnourished Omega stronger than she looked.

When she dared to set her teeth to his arm, Kieran slapped her hard enough to split her lip. He boxed her ear the moment she tried to pull out her IV and scramble away. And then in a voice so unlike the rage on his face, he calmly asked her why.

Shaking her head, feeling foreign food roil in her stomach, she begged with wide, wet eyes.

"Is it that you are afraid of needles?"

Confession was the only answer, one that was all the easier when a surprise prick of a needle left her floating on undulating apathy. Two blinks, a stuttering breath, and she let him press a pen into her fingers. Glancing at the sharp object, at the crumple of paper he pressed to her thigh, Wren coughed… and found it didn't hurt *that much.*

They had already been treating her *for days*. She already owed too much to ever pay when the bill came due.

Ink flowed over white paper. Paper with not even a dusting of dirt or a stain of mud. Paper that had not begun to mildew. *I'd rather be sick.*

Steely eyes took on a glint that didn't fit such beautiful features. "You'll die."

I can't pay! I can't go to the debtor's quarry. Not yet. My boys need me. I can die when they're old enough to take care of themselves.

The curl of Kieran's lip was not from

amusement, or even scorn. It was from absolute incomprehension, as if what she said was unfathomable. "You're not going to die, Jax."

Wren said nothing, only stared at him, her lip trembling despite the drugs. Of course she was going to die. Everyone died. Especially in the Warrens. She'd be lucky to live to thirty even with perfect health.

No one lasted. Everyone ended up buried in mud, weighted down with stone so their bodies did not float up once they started to bloat and decompose. Just like the children buried behind her home. Just like all her dreams. Tie a rock to it and let it sink deep, deep down.

The Second Alpha glowered, a look far too similar to Caspian's. "What good would you be to us sick? We take care of the girls in the pen. Caspian already spent a fortune on that special science muck he's been feeding you, and Toby's paying for your care. Me, I've been relegated to nursemaid… and believe me, I've got much better things to do than sit by the bedside of an ungrateful Omega."

Sit at the bedside? Had he been here all this time?

Sinking into the pillows, and there were many, Wren took notice. She was in her own room. There were no curtains dividing her from other sick patients. There was even a window showing a view she had not seen since her father tossed her out of his moving vehicle right into the stinking mud.

This wasn't a Warrens' shanty town clinic. The posh facility was midlevel, there was even a little bit of horizon between the tall buildings.

"Haven't seen it in a while, have you?"

It wasn't exactly as she remembered. Drab… it was drab, no less spectacular than the light reflecting off the morning mud down below. But it was light, and it did hold a certain appeal.

The shuck of a belt, the metallic click of the buckle, all ignored while Wren took in the view. Tooth by tooth, the sounds of a zipper descending, then the atmosphere grew full of a scent that softened the astringent air.

From the corner of her eye, Wren could see Kieran pumping his fist in a measured stroke down an impressive erection. Slow, the way she'd learned he liked it. Staring at her watching the view.

How he found any of this stimulating, she'd never know, but she met his heated gaze and held it.

"Right there, that fucking look in your eye is so goddamn hot."

What look? Resignation? But Wren was fooling herself. She'd been staring doe-eyed and full of nostalgia—maybe even wonder at that drab bit of sky. There had even been a soft smile playing at her lips as if this was her normal and she'd get to smile at the view every day.

She used to…

It hadn't been all bad with her family. There had been times it had even been… nice.

And she had never gone hungry.

Starvation and how to cope with it was something she'd learned in the Warrens.

In this moment, in this room, even if her body ached under the drugs, she wasn't hungry. Caspian had fed her. Kieran had bathed her. And Toby…

"Fuck… keep looking at me just like that." Fist dragging upward, he pulled foreskin over a swollen crown. His slit oozed, a thumb running a circle over the mess before Kieran reversed direction and stroked from tip to base.

He liked to watch. Apparently that extended to her just sitting still. But she let him, that view cascading over them both, holding his eyes as he fucked his hand and made enough noise anyone outside that door would know an Alpha was seeking pleasure.

Standing from his chair, cock and balls framed by an open zipper, Kieran closed the small distance between them. "You don't have to suck me, but I want you to swallow when I shoot my load. I want to be in your belly, sweet thing. Your first real meal that wasn't jammed down a tube." He took the back of her head, drawing her closer. "I can be gentle. Be a good girl and show me that you're grateful."

Spermy slime smeared her split lip. It stung, Wren unblinking as she met that gaze. And then he pushed inward, *gently*. Crown popping between her lips, the man managing to throw back his head, yet still hold her eyes.

Fist moving at a furious pace, he grunted in time with his hand.

Unsure why she did it, Wren gave a lick to the weeping slit staining her tongue. That was all it took, that one simple enticement before her cheeks flooded with flavor, and the Alpha groaned out a string of expletives— calling her a dirty slut no less than three times.

Cunt. Whore. Pretty, pretty tart.

That last one almost made her smirk.

It took several measured swallows to get

it all, to feel his spend coating her esophagus and churning in her belly. A portion dripped from the corners of her mouth, running down her neck to blemish the collar of her hospital gown. The Alpha didn't mind it one bit. Cock still bobbing in her face, he rubbed what leaked into her throat, sighing as if this was something he'd *needed*.

Maybe he had. A swallow from his fancy, dazed Omega set him at ease.

The doctor cleared his throat.

The connection was severed, Wren's cheeks hot with shame to realize another person been witness to whatever insanity was just shared between them.

Backs of his fingers ran over the bone of her cheek, Kieran chuckled to see her so undone. "It never lasts, this look. All the girls in the pen lose it in time, though sometimes they try to fake it, but I can always tell."

It never lasts because every last one of those women had been broken. It faded because those women were not loved, not by the males who kept them. Maybe even not by themselves.

Wren wanted to tell him this, but the pen and paper were gone, and unlike Toby, he had no interest in learning sign language. The Second may have been beautiful, maybe on some level he even thought his intentions were good—he certainly spoke in passion as if he did—but he was missing a fundamental piece of his soul.

Like Caspian, like charming, crazy Toby, Kieran was not a good man, and probably never had been.

And if she let them, the three of them would try to eat her until she was no different than jaded Rosie.

Caspian who stole her from her home. Kieran who liked to fuck her at her weakest moments. And Toby…

Her shoulder began to itch.

Absently scratching at the hospital gown, a gurgle of heartburn burned in her breast.

Abandoning her shoulder to press against her sternum, Wren winced.

The noise she made drew the attention of the two men. Both watched very closely, but it was the doctor who asked, "Are you in pain?"

She wasn't in anything, not with whatever drugs he'd pumped into her system, but she was *something*. Confused? Suddenly uneasy?

She'd played Kieran's game; she had submitted to his pack… and found oblivion speared by Toby's malformed cock. Pain, pleasure, all thoughts skidding to a mental halt until only the body existed and the mind had floated far away.

She let the Third do as he wanted with her, and her body had relished Toby's brand of defilement in its own way. Because Caspian had been holding her, and Kieran had watched over.

But, Toby must have damaged her badly enough that she ended up here.

God, her chest hurt. She could feel pain,

horrible gnawing pain no matter if she exhaled or held her breath. The room was spinning, the sounds of beeping machines fading into the hum of blood in her ears.

A pin light clicked, searing brightness burning through her pupil as the doctor forced open her lid. "She's going to pass out if he doesn't calm down."

"I'll deal with it." Again, Kieran gave her that look before he left the room.

Down the hall it sounded like something was breaking, shouts and roars. "I want to see her!"

The thumping pain redoubled until black crept through Wren's vision and all went quiet.

The next time she woke, Kieran was back, the catheter was gone, and a second IV port was in her other arm. "Breathing treatment first, then food. And if you submit like the good girl Caspian says you are, I'll take you to visit your boy."

She sucked in air from the misting cup

made to fit over nose and mouth. Without complaint, she ate a bowl of the same green sludge Caspian had fed her in her room. Sludge she now knew was more than food. It was alive, worked on the body from the inside out. Cost a fortune.

Because she was no good to them as a whore if she was sick.

And for some reason, she had woken up in a foul mood. Clearheaded, *finally*, she obeyed Kieran so that there would be no more injections or random swallows of creamy cum.

But bitterness tinged her actions. Wren had played their twisted sex games. She had kept her part of the bargain. And if Kieran didn't keep his and take her to Mikael, he was going to pay. All this was in her glare as she swallowed the last taste of sludge, and slammed down her spoon on the tray.

"Feisty."

Fuck you. Everyone knew that universal sign.

His attention piqued, Kieran raised a brow. It made him even more handsome, and made her even angrier.

"I can't tell if that's you or him, but I like it." He helped her up, his normally cold sneers replaced with an oddly chipper wink. "Don't be sore. I always keep my word. You can have your day with your boy."

And she did. She had the perfect day sitting on the edge of Mikael's bed and talking with someone she loved so much it hurt. She had a day of seeing him eat until he was full. A day of smiles.

A day to remember why she was doing this.

When Kieran told her it was time to go, she didn't argue or sneer. She smiled at the Second with real joy, and thanked him.

And obeyed.

Back in her room, despite the aches in her joints, she unhooked his buckle and let her unskilled fingers show him just how grateful she really was. She would be the best whore they ever had, please them in every despicable way so long as her boys were healthy and happy.

When Kieran growled and bent her over the bed, it wasn't like the last time in Caspian's room. He didn't hurt her or try to make her cry. The calculating caution he used when he shunted forward left her pushing back against him. She took his cock, sighing as he rocked her against the mattress.

Reaching under her hips to tease her clit with the soft stroke of a lover, Kieran brought her to orgasm in seconds. Wren kept her eyes open through the pitch and roll of pleasure, hissing at unexpected discomfort when his knot swelled to tie them into one.

She bore it looking out the window at a drab city and the sparking pink of a distant sunset as he shot his cum against her womb and pinched her clit until another wave of shimmering warmth left her milking his cock.

Praise was given with a kiss on the shoulder and long minutes of sure strokes down her spine. "My mom never looked at me the way you looked at that boy. She sold me for more crack in her pipe. It would have been nice to have been looked at like that."

Glancing over her shoulder at the Alpha standing between her dangling legs, Wren made the mistake of showing pity.

Kieran, more beautiful than one man should be, sneered. "Tell anyone I said that, and I'll kill you."

27

———————

It felt strange to be back in the pipeworks. This wasn't her home. The 'big room', as Rosie had called it, was unfamiliar in every way. Wren had only spent one disastrous day here, served Caspian, Kieran, and Toby *one night* before she'd woken in the hospital. And just like that was expected to nest here.

For now. In that brief encounter with Rosie, Wren had gleaned another key lesson. None of the girls were offered this room for long. Some of them coveted it.

Wren missed her true home, and knew it would not be long before Caspian found some new toy to play with and sent her packing. So long as Mikael was well, it would be a relief. This place made her skin crawl. As did the unfamiliar tapping in her chest.

A sign of the shrinking infection she hoped, but a sensation she was happy to see long gone.

One day she'd be able to forget about all of this. One day Caspian would fill her pockets with credits and send her off with a fortune in water. She'd be rich enough to see that both Mikael and Alec would have real futures away from the mud.

And that—that one dear thought—filled her heart with joy and made the stinking room bearable.

That… and she'd be remiss to pretend that finding new machines dotting the blank spaces between gaudy furniture in the *big room* wasn't also a little touching. Dehumidifiers, something that looked an awful lot like the contraption she been attached to for breathing treatments, and other things she couldn't account for… which considering her experience in salvage, was something to say.

It seemed the males really did want her to get better. Even if it was for their own selfish purposes, it made her feel like more than just a hole to fuck.

Kieran had carried her all the way from the hospital, pensive after their mating, to set her down in this transient place. He'd then ordered her to rest on that gross bed.

She had tried, but Wren was too…

Happy. Grateful. Hopeful for the first time in years?

There had been nothing in the world like watching Mikael talk about things he'd seen on the Cinema hologram. She'd never been able to provide anything but old junk she'd dug up, ancient tech, and now he had access to the panel in his room and the wonders people who mattered in the city enjoyed every day.

And now he wanted to star in holos.

Cute did not even begin to describe his enthusiasm.

Mikael was a good boy, but he'd never been a particularly optimistic one. And now he was going to be well; he was going to know the feeling of a full belly. He was going to thrive.

She'd make it happen no matter the cost.

She'd find him a place far away from the mud. Already a plan was forming. Caspian had promised her a year's worth of water when he was done. She would offer that with the boy to someone who could teach him a skilled trade. Someone would take him, train him; someone she got to hand-select.

Of course, they would take Alec too. That one wouldn't want to leave, there was too much of the wild thing in him, but she'd convince him. She had to.

The farther both of her boys were from The Syndicate the better. There was no future in the mud.

The ghosts of kids buried behind her house could speak to that. And Wren had sworn she'd never bury another. It wasn't in her. Not again.

Not ever.

Heart thrumming on this high, genuinely delighted, Wren ignored Kieran's order to rest and went to the small desk where paper and pen had been left for her use. The joyous minutes were filled with putting all that feeling onto paper.

Gratitude. An explanation of love. A promise.

Heartfelt letters written and folded.

Before she could contain herself, paper grasped in her fist, Wren threw back her door and rushed through the pipeworks so she might give them to Caspian herself.

Slaves—she would not mock their position by calling those mulling about paid workers—gawked at her. Several tried to grab, but she was fleet-footed and had a sense of where to go.

It was as if a glowing cord lead her right to him—a world of possibilities. Instinct.

That should have been her first warning.

Her heart sang. It led her to turn right, go down stairs, make a left, and scurry over some scaffolding. It called her forward past dangerous men marked with the black hand of The Syndicate, Wren's white drawstring pants and large borrowed shirt Kieran had dressed her in before leading her out of the hospital flapping at her back.

She could see the Alphas, all three of them gathered on the same deck where she'd gone to barter for her boys a week ago. She saw them and she smiled.

Toby's eyes glowed as if he'd waited just for her, already gazing in her direction in anticipation of her rush from the shadows. Toby, grinning despite a face pinched with many cuts and terrible bruising.

Was his arm in a sling?

It was. The sight of it slowed her feet to the point she almost tripped head over ass.

Instead that momentum kept her shuffling forward, her clumsy approach immediately noticed by the rest of the party on the platform.

Kieran gave a sharp shake of the head in a definite signal for her to leave at once, but Wren was determined: to thank the First who paid for Mikael's care. To thank the Third who saw that she'd been treated for a disease far worse then she'd suspected. Kieran had already been thanked with the willing use of her body and… what she suspected he really wanted. Wren had held him after the knot had diminished. She'd held him and purred, toying with his hair as she would have cuddled with her boys.

And because it was secret and because there had been no one to see, he had closed his eyes and reveled in it. For all his odd ways and his little cruelties, he might be the most damaged out of all Caspian's pack.

Yet there he was, glaring.

She would make this quick then.

On the catwalk ahead, Rosie hung on Caspian's arm, her blue summer dress splattered with rose print and unbuttoned down to her waist. That loud pattern was fitting, glamorous even, for a woman so beautiful. It showcased the perky breasts still on display, drew the eyes to dark nipples that jutted toward the mouth of the man bent over her.

Wren didn't need to sniff the air to know what ran down the Omega's thigh was Caspian's cum. He was still tucking himself away.

The stab that came with the sight, Wren would grow accustomed to. She didn't own these men. They owned her for a time. And so long as they kept their word, she would play their games and remember what this was.

Natural feelings were *unnatural* here. They were to be ignored and forgotten.

And so Wren tucked that unwarranted stab of sadness away and smiled all the larger.

It didn't matter that the other Omega hissed at her approach. It didn't matter that she reeked of Caspian, and even a little of

Kieran… whom Wren had given herself to less than an hour before.

Letters tight in her fist, Wren went to the First.

To the male who had stolen her.

To the first man who had told her she was not defective.

To a person she greatly feared and could never thank enough.

And slipped her arms around the stiff Alpha's middle to give him a genuinely heartfelt hug. She didn't even mind the hideous coat touching her, or the shock she sensed when he braced as if she'd burned him. She embraced him, her ear to his heart, and smiled as if all was right in the world.

He didn't purr. That was okay. She did, loudly, so loud it rang in her ears.

Pulling back, she went on quick tip toe and pressed a chaste kiss to his cheek before stepping back.

Eyes on her mouth, he scowled, dragging his thumb down her split lip. "What's this?"

Miming waking surprised and thrashing, she tried to get him to laugh. He didn't.

His loss.

Letters somewhat rumpled from her fist, she smiled at the male and held out the one with his name scratched on top. Pinching it from her fingers, face utterly blank, Caspian waited.

So she spoke in her way. Hands flowing with her excitement, Wren ignored all others to tell him exactly how she felt, knowing he could not understand, but hoping the sentiment came across.

Mikael is going to live thanks to you! Do you know what that means to me? There is nothing in the world I love more than my boys. Nothing. And today I saw my youngest smile, I saw him feel like he might have a shot at the world. I saw him come alive.

He laughed and it didn't hurt him.

Thank you! Thank you with all my heart!

I will repay this kindness. I swear it.

Glancing toward the seething Rosie, Wren

gave her a friendly smile, knowing she had interrupted time the other female prized with Caspian. Pressing her hands together in supplication, she wordlessly asked the Rosie's forgiveness for intruding. And backed away, still smiling.

The other Omega's disgust was obvious. "What the fuck is she doing here?"

"Shut up!" Caspian snapped at his *guest*, pulling open the letter to read it over. It didn't take him long to absorb the message or to turn rich brown eyes back upon the bearer.

They were furious. "You were told to rest! I forbid you from ever stepping foot down here again!"

The unexpected boom of his voice made Wren jump, avert her eyes in immediate submission, and back away. But she still had Toby's letter to pass forward, so she held it out, glancing quickly to where the Third edged forward.

Caspian snatched the paper from her hands, tore it lengthwise, and threw it over the ledge. Sailing end over end, the two halves were caught up by all the pouring water. Ruined.

Wren's eyes tracked the path, earlier exuberance melting into a chill when it fell into the churning cistern. Her page was caught up by clean water and washed down a path that led right where Wren had first entered Caspian's domain.

A figure far below was waving, face alive with excitement to see her. A boy with the painted black handprint of The Syndicate marking his face shouting, "Jax!"

Alec.

The boy she had bought with her body, jumping and exuberant to get her attention.

This… no…

Why was he here? Why marked as if he'd joined this band of criminals and murderers?

Like a snuffed out candle, the joy in her heart extinguished. Horror wormed its way into the hollow place, snapped through sinew and limb, and the icy clarity that she should have known better.

Daring to look at the seething male who'd forbidden her to come here, accusation sat clear on her face.

Caspian held no guilt in those mud colored eyes, only the glinting sting of entitlement. Clutched in his fist was her letter, a physical manifestation of her gratitude, and she could not help but stare at it as if it might come alive and destroy her.

Toby marched closer, speaking as if moving his jaw was difficult. "Go back to your room, sunshine. Now! I will come to you later."

This sinking feeling… this was what those who lived in the Warrens choked on every goddamn day.

Disappointment. Betrayal.

Wren looked to the Second. Kieran wouldn't even turn his head her direction.

She'd been dismissed.

As if these men had a right to do so.

They'd made an agreement, she'd held up her bargain… and it began to dawn on Wren that all the while, all those days, Alec had been right here. He'd probably marched right back to the pipeworks once she'd dragged him home and demanded a place.

And to get that mark, Caspian himself had accepted him into the fold.

Stolen him. LIED.

Caspian, Kieran, Toby… all of them had lied to her. Used her.

Churning behind her breast, swishing anger began to wash away sticky shame. It pushed it out her fingertips and into the air to coat the males who should be cursed to suffer it.

Teeth on edge, she cut a glare back to the eyes of her betrayer.

She could feel the veins pulsating behind her eyes, knew her nostrils flared and an intense look of hate shaped her face.

There had been times in Wren's life when she had felt anger. This was *so much more*.

Rage flowed through her spirit, and sent her dashing away. Rage moved her feet on a path not one of them might impede until she'd jumped off rotting planks, ran over crumbling cement, and swung her way down rickety ladders all the way below where the child laborers were whipped and abused.

Where *her* boy looked to now be in charge. Of innocent slaves. Of fellow people.

One look at his Jax, and Alec's enthusiasm became the sullen frown of a culpable accomplice.

The kid thought to placate. "I know what you're going to say…"

Wren struck him. And it was not the open-palmed slap of a mother correcting her young. It was the backhand of a pissed off Warrens' rat ready to harm.

Alec hit the floor with a yelp, pushing himself to scream, "You don't have a say in my life!"

Hands flying, Wren had her fucking say. *"Do you have any idea the things I've done so you wouldn't have to be here? DO YOU KNOW WHAT THEY DID TO ME?"*

"You've been put up special in the big room! Get anything you want." Sullen but loud in the way of embarrassed adolescent boys, Alec shoved her back and shouted, "Besides, the girls in the pen are taken care of!"

"HOW THE FUCK WOULD YOU KNOW?"

Dusting himself off and raising his chin, Alec boasted, "I'm a full member of the gang now. I've been there. It's nice. They have lots of food and water. Everyone smiles when they touch you."

She was going to be sick. He was a fucking boy already corrupted by this horrid place and the filth that gathered amidst so much clean water.

Seeing her pant, taking in the horrified whites of her eyes, Alec lost the smirk and cleared his throat. "Caspian is a great man—"

Never had she been so tempted to wrap her hands around Alec's throat and end him.

"He is not a great man. He's a criminal who enslaves the most vulnerable so he might climb higher on their corpses. And you want to be just like him?"

Stubborn, obstinate and angry, her boy, her sweet Alec spat. "Yes."

Wren hit him again, harder, knowing it would leave his ears ringing and linger in a bruise.

And while she reached for her kid's shirt, while she hoisted Alec up with unusual strength and shook him, Wren had heard the cause of all this pain rush forward.

It was their fault! She'd face down the males who had stolen her child and *ruined* him. Who'd ruined her!

Seething, glad her lungs could take on so much damp air, Wren dropped the kid they thought they might steal and turned her back on him to face down the enemy.

Ready to burst from her flesh, she snarled, hissed, and flexed her fingers. Water rained down upon them, soaking her white hair, her borrowed white clothes, and left them all filthy in its decadence.

Caspian, massive in his hideous coat of human flesh breathed fast and angry. He dared to glower at her as if she had broken their contract. As if *she* has threatened his family.

A year of water he'd promised her. Pockets full of credits. Two boys.

Bastard!

Behind him, Kieran held up his hand in caution. And Toby, that psychopath crooked his finger at her, calling out. "Come to me, darling girl. Step this way."

Never again.

Cracking his neck, Caspian crossed his arms over his broad chest, announcing, "Think of the other boy. It would be a shame if something—"

Color leached out of her vision, leaving greys and shadows, and a deep, abiding hate.

Wren didn't hear the rest of Caspian's speech or threats. How could she when a perfect piece of corroded rebar stuck out from the ancient cement, close enough that she might brace her foot against the ground and tear it out. Roaring, she hefted half the slab upward until it cracked. Watching the dust flake off her weapon, smiling to see a quantity of hardened rock still clung to the end of her perfect cudgel, she hoisted it high.

Caspian stood taller before his men, before his slaves, and demanded, "Put that down before you hurt yourself."

There would be pain alright. Theirs. She'd kill every last one of them.

And then he sealed his fate. "This farce of an agreement is behind us. You are mine, the boys are mine. Every last life in this fucking city is mine. Don't think I won't hesitate to harm the other one if you don't obey."

The other one? This bastard didn't even know the name of the boy he threatened.

Animal noises came from her chest, a mournful wheeze twisted in a raw, chattering growl.

There was a point all males knew not to push an Omega past, a point that led to unyielding bloodlust. She became something else.

A creature that would single-mindedly defend her young. A creature who could not feel pain. A creature who would not stop until death.

She was going to kill this man, beat him to death with the metal rod she'd torn from hardened rock.

"Stop threatening her boy, boss!" Toby pushed forward, snapping his teeth at Caspian before his wild eyes met her unblinking gaze. "Put down the weapon and come to me, mate. Mikael will remain unharmed. You have my word."

Mate? Her grip tightened about the aged rebar, fingers going white. That word? Worthless.

Cajoling, singsonging false calm, Toby held up his hands patting air as if to calm her. "This is all a misunderstanding. Look, he even gave Alec a place. One with pay. Food. Water. You'll be able to keep a close eye on him. Caspian means no harm to your boys."

"Like hell I don't!" The First Alpha stripped off his disgusting coat, dropping it to the mud, muscles bulging as he demanded surrender. *"Submit, now*, or I'll cast him out on the street. Submit, or the sick one will drown in his own body's juices. You are mine! I don't give a fuck about our agreement."

Greys and shadows bleached away until her world was only black and white.

Rearing back with a guttural scream, Wren launched herself at the betrayer, laughing at his roar.

28

Lashes crusted and gummed with drying blood stuck together when Wren tried to blink herself awake. The ground below her was cold and wet. She was soaked, naked, save for scraps of ruined cloth and the icy touch of heavy chains.

They weighed her down, pinning her to that rough cement floor.

There was enough light coming through the crack in the door to see her shackled hands and swollen, stiff fingers. Five of her nails had been torn off. At least three of her fingers were broken… and the blood. Her skin was scraped off.

Wren could see why. She'd attacked the door, the walls… herself.

Around the shackles on wrists and ankles was raw skin, torn when she'd tried to remove them.

She didn't remember doing it. She didn't remember being chained or thrown in this room.

All she could remember was Caspian's threats. *Submit, now, or I'll cast him out on the street. Submit, or the sick one will drown in his own body's juices.*

Well now she was lying in hers. Everything hurt: each muscle, each bone. Her split flesh.

So many bites marked her limbs. They burned, but nothing like the gouged flesh of her neck. Raw fingers had tested the skin, coming away bright red. She was still bleeding, just as her cunt still spilled cum if she moved.

It smelled of Caspian.

These were his bites. He had bruised her and torn her neck. And she could remember *nothing*.

He should have just killed her and been done with it. Shoving her into a dark closet to rot seemed too personal.

It was almost as if he *cared*.

That thought made her laugh, a thing she regretted immediately when scabbing skin stretched and oozed. If he thought to torture her, he'd better hurry. Infection would kill her in a matter of days.

Maybe this was Caspian's idea of compassion. Time to mourn her boy before inevitable death carried her out of this hellish life.

Footfalls outside her door, the shadow of a man, and Wren began to sob. They could do whatever they wanted to her so long as she was reunited with Mikael and Alec in the afterlife.

And maybe, just maybe, the First was

bleeding now too.

Hopefully they all were. Caspian, Kieran, Toby… damn them all to burn in hell.

The iron crank of a rusted lock shrieked, encroaching light burning her eyes as the door parted and a man peered in.

"Are you sane?"

Considering the one who asked, Wren hiccupped—an almost laugh in all her misery.

Toby peered in at her, the look on his bruised face setting a thump in her chest that almost knocked the wind from her lungs.

"I don't blame you, sunshine." He slipped through the door, closing it behind them so just the two of them were sequestered in the shadows. Kneeling, he lifted her shivering body so she might rest against his chest and steal warmth. "I don't blame you, but I do *request*…"—he spoke the word as if testing it. As if really wanting to say demand instead —"Yes, I *request* that you capitulate. You cannot win, sweet girl. You must apologize."

He smoothed sticky hair from her face,

staring down at what must be horrible damage with a frown.

"So pretty…"

Teeth chattering—and yes, her tongue felt all of them—Wren could offer up only another sorry sob.

"Beg him for the lives of your boys. Do it now before it's too late."

That got her attention.

Despite the wreckage of her fingers and her bleeding wrists, Wren tried to grasp the front of his shirt. A shirt already marked with her blood, sweat, and tears.

"We will get past this, all of us." He pressed a kiss to her aching forehead. "But only if you submit."

Nodding emphatically, Wren gagged on the gore in her throat and tried to sign.

She would not be signing for some time. Truly mute, tears fell, the salt stinging as they ran their course.

He held her eyes, purring as if the sound

might set her at ease. "Someday I hope you'll tell me what that letter said."

Before she might find a way to reply, he stood, hauled her up into his arms, chains and all, and carried her sorry, half-frozen body out of the dark.

It was a short walk to Caspian's room, Wren noting that his hive seemed oddly silent. Beyond the sound of rushing water there were no yelps from whipped slaves, no barked orders from evil men. Just the water, the thrum in her chest, and the sound of Toby's breathing.

Two guards flanked the door, one opening it without so much as a glance at the bloodied, naked woman. And then she was inside.

It struck her how familiar the space had become. The scents swept through her nostrils, invaded her lungs, and set that constant throb in her chest to spiraling heights.

Caspian waited. Kieran too.

The pair of them stood in the center of the space, but Wren couldn't make out their expressions. She was too busy enjoying the wounds exposed by fresh clothes.

Even in all her pain, in all that desperation, she enjoyed that Caspian's eyes had both been blackened. That the corners of his mouth were crusted with blood. Under his clothes she pictured long strips of missing flesh, maybe even one of her missing fingernails burrowed deep to prick and harm.

These were evil thoughts. That man, that hateful, vile, deceiver had the lives of her boys in his hands, and though her chest thumped, her lips blubbered.

This awful person wanted her to scrape at his feet. He *owned* them all. His word meant nothing.

But he was her only chance.

Ground met her knees, Toby laying her naked, chain-draped body at the feet of his master.

Thoughts of Mikael smiling from his hospital bed, the sound of his laughter ringing clear with no tinge of a wheeze, and Wren broke.

Just like all the women in these caverns.

Clinging to his boot, lips pressed the laces, she wept a river of pain and begged.

Kieran's scent neared until paper and pen were laid beside her.

"Write that you are mine," Caspian demanded, draping the ultimatum in a seductive purr.

Manacled wrists moved together to pick up the pen, fumbled it, and tried again. It took agonizing ages to gather it in a fist only three fingers could grasp. Even longer to try to scratch upon the page, *Please don't hurt my boys*.

"Then submit." He crouched over her bent head, a hand tangling in her wet hair. "Write it."

The sounds that came from her as she penned his demand were pathetic, angry, horrible… but she did as he requested, that hand on her head oddly supportive.

I'm yours.

"You are." His fist tightened in her hair, gathering the mass back so he might yank her head upward to expose the worst of her wounds.

Her throat, she felt fresh blood pump from the open wound to trickle warm down so much cold skin.

"Look at me."

Lavender eyes tracked over massive legs, a belted waist. They dragged over the fresh shirt that hugged a muscled stomach, flexed pectorals to a neck that had the tiny, swollen bite of a female mouth. He pulled her hair all the tighter until she met a gaze full of something she could not name.

Thumb swiping her tears, Caspian purred. "I was extremely impressed with your strength, little mouse."

The unwelcome beat in her chest pulsed, shook her, and sent another escaped drip of Alpha cum to trickle from her pussy.

"It took hours to tame you and I enjoyed every last fucking minute."

Fucking. Because he had fucked her raw.

He knelt even lower, pulling her ear to his lips. "And so did you, pretty mouse."

Thank you for reading BRANDED. I hope you loved Wren and the Alphas who've claimed her! Read SILENCED now!

SILENCED
Wren's Song, Book Two

"She is not to feel pain."

A command like broken glass grinding into an open wound. Sharp, gouging—the kind of abrasive threat that would make a grown man feel Death breathe down his neck.

The physician's hands stuttered, his work dabbing blood from mangled fingers faltering. Such hesitation betrayed much more than the Beta's anxious scent. This was a male who knew one wrong word would see him a corpse. "I'm afraid that is impossible, sir."

Hovering overly close, Caspian snarled. "What did you just say to me?"

In the short minutes since the physician had begun examining his captive mouse, the First Alpha's fine mood had decayed. Raging victory at her chicken-scratched promise of loyalty faded. The glory that had beaten through his chest upon seeing her pale flesh marked by his many bites, depleted.

The ruby-red rivulets of blood that ran from the garish wound where his teeth had pierced her throat were no longer beautiful.

The glassy-eyed albino was a fucking wreck—one stuttering exhale away from the reaper.

Keeping an unwavering eye on his prize, Caspian put a hand on her ankle, one of the few places on her body that was not damaged, as he addressed the frazzled Beta physician who'd been dragged from his bed in the middle of the night.

"*No Pain!* And no scars will remain." This he could give her, stroking his thumb over the protrusion of her ankle bone. "Do you understand me, doc? Only the bite on her neck is to be left alone."

From where he paced beside the bed, Toby issued a challenging growl. Clipped words followed a twitch in his cheek. "My claiming mark will remain on her shoulder, Caspian. Do you hear me? Remove it, and you force me to bite her again."

Chest expanding in an angry breath, Caspian was cut short when the physician interjected. "Gentlemen, I cannot erase this kind of damage with a handheld cauterizing laser. All of these wounds will scar, though I will do my best to keep it minimal. But skin cell manipulation requires delicate application of the larger equipment in my clinic, days of careful monitoring, possible surgery depending on the depth of the damage. She should be brought—"

The very idea inspired pulsating fury in Caspian's chest, a cage of unbending black encasing a shriveled, beating organ. "Suggest taking the Omega from this den again, and I'll slit your throat."

One threat against the old man, and Caspian's mouse finally turned her head. Their eyes met, muddy brown to bloodshot violet, and a look of such heartbreak took her from vacant to wretched. It said, *please*. It urged the target of that glance to settle and be calm.

One thing it did not do was challenge; not that look. The mouse gave him a look of complete and miserable surrender.

Where had the warrior gone? The mouse brave enough to face his brawn with little more than a bent piece of cement-caked rebar?

Where was the hellion who'd taken his leaking cock with a scream, bucking her hips to pull him deeper even as she'd tried to throw him off?

What of the Omega who had set her teeth to his throat, and dared mark him as if she might claim ownership?

How she had howled and spat curses with her eyes. How she'd choked on Toby's then Kieran's cocks, guzzling down their cum once knotted and trapped beneath Caspian's full weight.

He'd filled her to the brim with seed, forced her to hold it all in so it might swim around her belly and let the fiery thing know she was outmanned. And still she'd fought, grinding Caspian's knot deeper, howling her rage as that perfect cunt fluttered and sucked.

Caspian had fucked her every possible way, knotted her more times in those maddening hours than he'd ever taken a woman. It wasn't about keeping her pinned. It was about filling her with more, forcing submission upon the hellcat who had, without question, bruised several of his ribs and torn several pretty gashes into his skin.

The urge to get more cum inside her, to sink his teeth into the wriggling, vicious mouse's flesh… he'd been drunk on it. High on her scent, intoxicated with the strangling grip of her pussy.

On the broken thing's strength.

He'd fucked her face down, scraping her tits over old, wet cement. Flipped her over once the first knot shrunk and shoved his way back in so he might see her blown eyes when he brought her to another ragged climax. All claws and teeth, she'd also taught him that a little Omega severed from sanity was as dangerous as she was fun.

Volleys of blows had struck his temple. But when his little mouse went for the eyes…

Had he been weaker, he would now be blind.

Delicate fists were trapped, but only after she'd broken his nose. Sent him roaring as he knotted her a third time and fucked her into a pulp while his men were in a riot of applause. Hundreds saw. The Syndicate, their slaves… the females daring enough to leave the pen and gawk.

They saw him maul his prize. Saw her disarmed, subdued, and ridden.

And their ovation fed Caspian's beast.

Kieran and Toby savored his kill as well. Just as pack should.

They got the remains the monster within deigned to share.

They got her throat.

The same throat Caspian had torn with his teeth. That *need* had gripped him, demanding all who'd borne witness see that the hissing viper was *his,* no matter whose cock she swallowed.

Kieran had been the one to take her by the hair so Toby's prick could be shoved between her gnashing teeth.

She'd bitten him good, of course. The sick fuck had gotten off on it, cumming almost immediately and swamping her cheeks with spermy cream. Whatever tension had been brewing between Alphas Two and Three was obliterated when she sputtered and coughed, following that pathetic moment by licking her lips and opening wide for more.

Kieran dipped in, Toby tending to his Second's prostate with a clever finger and words of encouragement.

This was seen by the Syndicate. They saw all three Alphas who ruled them united in victory.

They saw an Omega of amazing capability cowed and owned by her betters.

A glorious, violent mating—truly worthy of his pack.

But even then, the insane little guttersnipe had not submitted. All saw her wriggle her way out of their embrace to seek out a new weapon, and then to scream when the Omega could not find her adopted child.

Before she had been violent. In that instant, she went stark raving mad.

The wiry teenager had been dragged away by wiser members of his gang the moment he'd been stupid enough to beg Caspian for mercy for his *mom*.

Dragged off like the child he was, denied the view of his guardian's interminable and violent rebirth. And that would follow him through the years in the gang.

Once sworn, these males had only one allegiance.

The Syndicate swore fealty, abandoned family, gave all to their leader.

They didn't cry or beg for mercy.

Alec had failed his first test of loyalty, and would be brutally punished.

He'd missed the glory of the men's cheering—the blood the mouse had drawn from Kieran, Toby, and even Caspian.

In his sobbing state and begging pathetic wailing, he'd missed the glory of an Omega's whirlwind of violence and lust.

God, the pretty mouse's fierce subjugation had been beautiful.

Where she kept that side of herself when mellow and docile, Caspian could never guess. But seeing her unleashed, even just the once, was enough to slake a thirst he'd never known he might possess.

He'd jerk off to the look on her face when he first fucked into her dripping cunt for years. Feel her flesh between his teeth, the taste of her blood and his on his tongue.

The way she'd roared…

But now, after a full and proper capitulation, he did not feel vindicated.

He looked at the little Omega holding his eyes and felt a simmering disquiet.

Damage. Pain. Wounds that would scar.

Broken fingers the best doctor in Dale City was struggling to set.

A female who reeked of loss. Not joy. Not the epiphany of being owned by strong males.

One who suffered.

A grinding, soul-deep moment of realization sunk in. These were not just bite wounds. *Caspian had marked the mouse*. He could still feel the squish of her breaking skin in his teeth, was already eying the unmarked ankle he caressed as if ready to set his teeth to that snowy patch of skin.

And he had chomped down so many times she would be scarred with the crescent shapes of his enthusiasm for life.

Across the bed, Toby continued to pace, no longer replete or satisfied from fucking her mouth. "You should not have threatened her boys."

Drawing up to full height, Caspian

cracked his neck and at long last broke the stare he'd shared with the mouse. "Are you not proud of your mate?"

Palms slapping the mattress, rocking it enough that the Omega winced when her body shifted, Toby bellowed, "She's your mate now too! Look at her fucking neck! At her arms, her tits. What part of her did you not maul?"

Only the slender ankle under Caspian's stroking thumb. That was the only place that had somehow been spared in their battle.

A corkscrew of needle sharp sensation rocked Caspian back on his heels, mud brown eyes darting back toward the woman whose gaze was not shut to him. But that was not what held his attention. Bubbling antibiotic foam had been sprayed over the gouges in her neck, dripping a fizzy pink mess down her filthy chest.

Watching it, knowing the reason she bore such wounds, left his overused prick so hard it sawed at the zipper of his pants.

Kieran, arms crossed over a scratched chest, let out the most disappointed of breaths. "You marked her, yes. Get it out of your system before she hits estrous. Fuck her, fill her, knot her, whatever. Then wash your hands of this madness before we lose face."

Toby, veins in his neck throbbing, seethed. "You got hard and marked her with cum, just like the rest of us."

"But I never bit her!" Scrubbing a hand over his jaw, Kieran looked away from his First as if ashamed. "Cunts of all flavors are just down the hall. Females who desire nothing more than to please. You cannot trust one womb! She tried to kill you and you *marked* her for it!"

A hundred women, maybe more, waited in the pen to suck his cock with gusto on demand.

To debase themselves and do filthy things just for a moment of his attention.

And this mouse was practically a virgin. Unskilled. In no way eager.

Hated him.

And this little slip of girl is the one he'd bonded to in a passion.

Estrous or not, that foreign pining in his chest—the infectious pain—she was the cause!

The Beta doctor cleared his throat, swallowed, and began to set the bones in her other swollen, gnarled hand.

The Omega didn't so much as blink. By all appearances her lavender-rimmed pupils told the story of a bitch in heat. But it was all a lie.

Warm, salty tears marked her blood-speckled cheeks. A deep sense of loss resonated through her spirit straight into Caspian's heart.

His pretty mouse—the utterly still, wrecked girl—grew so far lost in her thoughts, it was as if she didn't notice how the doctor manipulated her joints, the pricks of his needles, or the steady stream of Toby's obnoxiously loud purr.

For all appearances, she felt no physical pain.

But it was a lie. Those violet eyes were clouded by hurt. She even inadvertently shrank when Caspian leaned over her to draw in a long analytical sniff.

He'd threatened the doctor so now she would not so much as whimper.

Fussing like a smitten schoolgirl, Toby grabbed a discarded pillow and fluffed it, adding it the makeshift nest he'd been building around her for the last hour. All of his efforts smeared with blood and reeking of Omega fear.

Knee to the mattress, he smooshed that pillow into place so she was cocooned in Caspian's bedding, his voice suddenly soft. "There you go, my sunshine."

A bonded male smitten with his mate.

One who practically vibrated with possession.

One who overstepped himself when he grabbed a creamy thigh, gently prying the

Omega's legs open. There, for the whole room to see was a cock-battered cunt that still seeped Caspian's seed.

Between pretty, swollen labia oozed a pearlescent trail of male conquering.

Of domination.

As if he had the right, Toby reached forward and scooped up a palm-full of leaking cum. A moment later that same hand was smeared against the gaping wounds on the pretty mouse's neck—rubbed in while Caspian roared.

The Third was flung across the room, Caspian pressing his female down into his mattress. Like a maniac he licked that cum from her wound. Cleaning his mate while offering a comforting purr.

Tongue fully outstretched, he caught himself.

Under him she was utterly still, oddly pliant.

Notched between her bruised thighs, cradled in the shape of her body, Caspian said the words before he could stop himself. "We could come to a compromise, you and I."

Though she seemed asleep, the Omega rattled.

"Show me you're willing to play by my rules, and I'll keep my fierce little mouse."

It wasn't a compromise he sought, no matter the words. He wanted something she was utterly unwilling to offer.

The Omega didn't want him. She didn't want Toby. And Caspian suspected she loathed Kieran. But that thing caging the organs in his ribs hungered for more than her surrender.

"Be a good girl for me until your next estrous. Play house and please. Give me all an Omega owes her Alpha, and I will set your boys free."

For all that she moved, she might as well have been asleep. She judged his word as valueless.

Listing his demands, Caspian began with, "I will fuck other women."

Not so much as a flinch.

Irritated that she believed she could ignore him, Caspian licked at her lips. "Sometimes I'll want those women to fuck you while I watch."

Read SILENCED now!

ADDISON CAIN

USA TODAY bestselling author and Amazon Top 25 bestselling author, Addison Cain's dark romance and smoldering paranormal suspense will leave you breathless. Obsessed antiheroes, heroines who stand fierce, heart-wrenching forbidden love, and a hint of violence in a kiss awaits.

For the most current list of exciting titles by Addison Cain, please visit her website: addisoncain.com

facebook.com/AddisonlCain

bookbub.com/authors/addison-cain

goodreads.com/AddisonCain

ALSO BY ADDISON CAIN

Don't miss these exciting titles by Addison Cain!

Standalone:

Swallow it Down

Strangeways

The Golden Line

The Alpha's Claim Series:

Born to be Bound

Born To Be Broken

Reborn

Stolen

Corrupted

Wren's Song Series:

Branded

Silenced

The Irdesi Empire Series:

Sigil

Sovereign

Que (coming soon)

Cradle of Darkness Series:

Catacombs

Cathedral

The Relic

A Trick of the Light Duet:

A Taste of Shine

A Shot in the Dark

Historical Romance:

Dark Side of the Sun

Horror:

The White Queen

Immaculate

www.ingramcontent.com/pod-product-compliance
Lightning Source LLC
Chambersburg PA
CBHW061219190726
48288CB00001B/241